The Harvester

Princess Sky Xera Nerezsh came to earth to avoid the normal succession to the throne. Being the oldest daughter, she will be required to murder her mother in order to secure her path to power. Sky loves her mother and refuses this way, choosing instead to disappear in the vast reaches of space. When her past collides with her present, she must think quick on her feet, claim two men and a whole planet just to avoid the inevitable: a meeting with her mother. Along the way, she discovers true love and a burning need to be there for them always. Now if the other Harvesters can just keep to themselves, they'll have no problems. But who said true love was ever easy.

Other Books By Lynn Crain

eXtasy Books/Devine Destinies
The Haunting of Maggie Grey (eBook)
Shopping Spree (eBook)
Captive Illusions Series (eBook)
      Iain and Kelsey
Orchid Series (all eBooks)
      Fluke
      More Than Robotics
Santa's Elves Series (all eBooks)
      The View From Santa's Sleigh
      The Thing About Elves
      An Elf's Desire
      A Love For Eggther
      An Elf's Magic
      Giselle's Elf
      An Elf's Love
      Santa's Miraculous Christmas (December 2016)
Santa's Elves (print of Santa's Elves Books 1-3)
Subtle Invasion (eBook)
To Take An Apprentice (eBook)

MuseItUpHOT!
An Oasis in the Desert – Lacey's Lamp series (eBook)

Shooting Star Books (eBooks)
A Lover for Rachel
A Viennese Christmas
Night of the Blue Moon ~ Blue Moon Magic Series
The Harvester

World Romance Writers (eBooks & print)
Letterbox Love Stories
Holiday Magic (December 2016)

The Harvester

By

Lynn Crain

First Print Publication: December 2016

The Harvester
Copyright © 2012 Lynn Crain

ISBN10 1-62052-033-8
ISBN13 978-1-62052-033-8

Cover Art by Su Kopil, Earthly Charms

Published by Shooting Star Books
www.shootingstarbooks.com

For My Wonderful Readers...

And as always...Gordon...thanks for letting me do my thing.

Prologue

IT HAD NEVER BEEN her intent to be at odds with her mother. The gods knew her mother was a formidable opponent and no one in their right mind would want to stand against that woman, least of all her. Life at home had gotten increasingly hard, so hard Sky knew she had to get out on her own or she'd never get the chance again.

"Are you sure this is what you want to do?" The fierce look on her mother's face would make anyone tighten in fear.

"Absolutely, Mother. You told me I would have to make my way someday. I chose to do this now and in this manner. Is that a problem?"

Her mother's eyes narrowed. "Not really, Daughter, but I do wonder if your motivation is something more. You are my oldest and my expectations for you are different than your sisters."

She tried hard not to swallow because any weakness shown on her part could make her request denied. Instead, Sky gave a tight smile. "Nothing more than the need to be on my own for a while. Surely, you understand that need. It is my hope my sisters will more than make up for my absence." She'd heard the stories over and over again where her Mother asked her

Grandmother for some freedom and that freedom had been denied more than once. Her Mother told her daughters repeatedly, she would never deny them such a basic need.

Her Mother returned the gesture and patted her shoulder. "I understand, Daughter. I will expect to hear from you at regular intervals."

She bowed her head. "Understood. Are there any other instructions you might have for me?"

The Queen shook her head. "Not really. Just pick up a standard packet before you leave. And good journey." The woman drew her close and placed a kiss on her cheek. "I expect to hear good things from and about my Daughter."

Never having her Mother show any affection, she kept her surprise to herself. As far as she could tell, daughters were only good for political maneuvering. "Thank you, Mother." She returned the kiss and backed away. "I won't disappoint you." Sky did a full bow and backed out of the room completely before turning to make her way down the hall in slow, sure steps.

Her happiness was hard to contain, as she understood she was free to pursue her own agenda. Free of her Mother's overbearing manner. Free of her insufferable rules and regulations on how one should live their life. As she walked down the corridor, she made her plans, plans that didn't include any of her Mother's teachings or wants or desires. Sky knew the moment she was able, she would drop completely off her mother's radar.

Then, her life would really begin.

••••✳••••

Chapter 1

Sᴋʏ Nᴇʀᴇᴢꜱʜ ꜱᴄᴀɴɴᴇᴅ ᴛʜᴇ room in hopes of seeing just why the woman was here to see this particular show instead of an early one. While it hadn't taken long to get Angela Mather and her friend Dot Gentry on her radar, she was surprised that the normally classy young woman dressed in a plain and dowdy outfit. Nothing about her or her friend spoke to the wealth their families possessed. She made a quick note of the exits and anything else she might need should she have to get her target out of here in a hurry since this young woman could easier cause a scene.

Even more strange was she and her friend Dot called themselves Cher Horowitz and Gentry Jones. Sure, her boss, Avery Mather, had told her the girl had taken the news she was never to see Jinx McCoy again hard, even more so when he told her he would cut her off financially if she didn't start doing what she was told and get her college degree. But resorting to dressing like a nun was farfetched even for her and if her breath was any indication, she'd drunk herself silly before she came. Sky glanced at Angela's friend who merely shrugged and returned her gaze to the stage and their surroundings as if sizing the place up herself.

·•••✳•••·

Angela appeared to be planted for the moment which allowed her to reflect a minute on their connection to Avery Mather. When he'd called this evening she should have let the darn phone ring when his number streamed across the digital display as she had plans. She had felt obligated to answer his call and comply with his wishes. She'd been one of his faithful employees for nearly eight years and never missed his call.

Obligated. The very word carried weight and she didn't use it lightly. The man had been a savior when she needed one. If he'd been a younger man, she might have fancied him herself but Avery was happily married with children and grandchildren, hence her very reason for being here. He'd taken her under his wing, teaching her everything she needed to know about the bodyguard business on this blue-green planet on the edge of its galaxy when no one would take her serious. The relationship had lasted longer than some marriages in this town known as Sin City on the third rock from their star.

The lights dimmed a little as she returned to the task at hand. She'd have time to ponder her life here later. Right now, she needed to understand just what Angela planned. Avery said that whatever she did, it couldn't reflect bad on the family or its casino holdings. If it did, she would be out on her ear within minutes of Sky's report to him. She felt a moment of trepidation as she wondered if the girl even knew just how close she was to being tossed out on her own without her trust fund.

She crossed her arms and gave a brief glance to each of the occupants at the table. Besides Angela and her friend Dot, there were a couple of tourists consisting of a curly-haired blonde guy, a small redhead and an older woman who appeared to be in her sixties or seventies, all of which were seated across from her. On her side of the table, sat an auburn-headed woman, who appeared very excited and a more relaxed dark-haired gal, who seemed to be enjoying herself immensely, seated immediately next to her.

As if on cue, the last lady leaned forward and across the redhead, card in hand. "Hi, I'm Jayne Morrow, reporter for the Las Vegas Tribune. I'd like to get your opinion on the show later if I may."

Sky was taken aback as normally other women didn't speak to her often, her size and stance too intimidating she supposed. Then again, maybe it was the all black outfit. In essence, women avoided her while men seemed to want to fuck her. "Uh – sure – if you really want my opinion."

Her deep voice could be heard over the din of the other women in the room. Many had told her the sound held the throatiness and seduction of either Lauren Bacall or Kathleen Turner both famous actors. She wouldn't know as she'd never seen either on the rare occasions when she watched TV or went to a movie. She agreed with those who felt the media a mindless pit of unproductiveness compared to the bigger picture.

"Honey, I want everyone's opinion. After all, women want to see men who are attainable in a show and definitely not gay – know what I mean?" Her smile rang true and the female had an aura of trustworthiness found in few on this planet.

Gay? She hoped her confusion didn't show on her face. Gay didn't mean happy the way this woman was using it. Earth languages were so confusing at times and it took her years to understand even the most basic nuances. It had to mean – "Ah, yes, I understand what you mean." She nodded as she finally got the context meaning the males didn't prefer other males.

Angela took that moment to jump up from her chair and glide across the floor to the bar line in such a way others tend to ignore. She narrowed her eyes, aligning her optics to see if she could read the girl's lips as the simply dressed woman barely chatted with those around her. Returning her gaze to the woman seated across from her, she smiled and asked, "Have you ever been to one of these things before?"

There was a brief moment of fear in the redhead's eyes across from her and she realized her mistake too late. "Contacts," she stated matter of fact.

"But – but – your eyes are glowing. And there's things that look like they're whirling in there." Confusion was plain on the woman's face.

Sky gave a wry smile and shook her head. "Yeah – I put in a wrong contact order and got a box of glow in the dark ones. As for the movement, I guess they are moving around on my eye. I think they don't quite fit correctly."

The man next to her frowned. "I've never heard of those before."

"They're the rage of all the teenagers now apparently." She understood that her optic enhancements would have to stay in place the entire time she was at this table or there would be more questions. It was so easy to let her guard down and forget she wasn't home any more where everyone had some sort of enhancement. Not that she wanted to be home. In all honesty, home was more foreign than this planet had ever been, which was the reason she left in the first place.

Though she wanted to sigh her frustration out loud for both the situation and her mistake, she held a tight rein on her reactions. She didn't need to bring any more attention to herself. It could cause suspicion and the boss man had informed her the whole operation was to be on the sly. He was sure no one knew Angela was going to the show except her best friend Dot. He found out only when one of his spies at the Camelot called to let him in on her planned activities for the evening. It was obvious the man didn't think Jinx McCoy was worthy of his daughter.

Angela slipped into her seat once again and gave her friend an exotic looking drink while sitting down another for herself along with two bottles of water. Drinking dulled one's senses and Sky couldn't afford to be lax in her duty so she opted for water when she arrived, thankful she still had a full bottle left. Her eyes narrowed again as she tried to guess what was in the quiet little blonde's head because the woman took only dainty sips from her drink even though it was obvious she had been drinking prior to her arrival. She smiled again at those at the table and tried to shelve the feeling she should drag the woman out by the scruff of her neck, kicking and screaming.

The room finally went dark and the music blared loudly, shaking the glasses at the bar. Sky perceived movement in her chest as the noise reverberated off the walls. The lights ushered in a line of men all in chain mail as a multitude of colors lit the stage. Soon they were gyrating to the beat of the song. The men of this world didn't command her attention in normal situations but this was...different...and brought long buried memories of another lush world and her dealings with it filtered into her mind.

Texra had been a slave port for eons where one could find anything they wanted no matter what the species or darkest desire. Trouble was she hadn't wanted anything when her foot stepped across the threshold of the second-rate spaceport located on the twilight side of the planet. She'd gotten more than she bargained for that last time her mother sent her there. The memories, while good and bad, needed to stay where they were...in the past.

Her attention was immediately drawn back to the present as a thunderous roar echoed through the large space. Her training kicked in as her hand reached for her weapon as her drazee slid to her palm. Her eyes went to those across the table from her and the others in the room as she found them all cheering or clapping and realized it was part of the show's opening act as some minor pyrotechnics made the even louder sounds.

As she steadied her breathing, she allowed herself the luxury to really look at the men on the stage. They all were very good looking but only the dark-haired ones caught her eye with two men in particular as they stood side-by-side on the left of the main dancer who she knew to be Jinx McCoy. She allowed her optics to kick in yet again in a way as not to alarm the others and scanned their faces closer. One had almost violet eyes while the other had eyes the color of the sky on Octa. One was nearly clean-shaven and the other had a bit of scruff, which she found incredibly appealing. In addition, both were taller than her six-foot frame. She swallowed hard because she knew on Texra, these types of dances were what were expected of the slaves up for auction as they performed for their very lives. Those two men would command a high fee because their bodies were hard and made for sex while their faces were very pleasant to look upon.

Suddenly, this seemed like a very bad idea as she fought to control herself. Everyone in the room whooped and hollered their encouragement for what each of the men on stage did to entice them. She could tell they wanted more...hell...she wanted more and wished she had room to cross her long legs under the table. Closing her eyes, she willed her urges down, as now was not the time for indulgence. She felt so hot and cold as her senses swam. She could make out their subtle scent at this distance and it was all she could do to keep her emotions in check as her mind warred with her body and what she could do with those males who caught her attention. It was these senses that made her her mother's best Harvester.

Riley, the emcee, introduced them all and stepped back from the line to allow the main dancer, Jinx, take center stage. He immediately ripped the chain mail from his body and gripped his crotch in what seemed to be a single move. Sky glanced toward Angela and saw the thin line of her lips as the emotions seemed to roll across her face. This didn't bode well but she could hardly tackle the woman in full view of everyone in the auditorium. In the next moment, he pulled off his pants, revealing a red G-string and Sky thought the woman would explode on the spot.

Undergarments of all kinds floated past her head as the women of the audience threw them toward the stage the moment they spied the man's package. She bit off her snort of laughter because she could see Angela was not amused but getting more frustrated by the minute as a tear slid out the corner of her eye.

Not good, not good at all. Sky had to figure out something fast or this situation would get out of hand in a very short time.

Before she could get her plan aligned, Angela got up and went to a spot before the stage, standing and looking at the man on stage as he danced. When he didn't come to even look at her, she stomped back to her chair amid the yelling from the crowd to get back to her seat. She never even heard Jinx tell Riley to get handcuffs and a bucket of ice water as he clamped his arms around her before she sat back down.

Sky gave a brief look at Dot who grinned broadly. Clearly, the woman thought that Angela would get what she deserved. As she rubbed the spot on her forehead between her eyes, she knew it to be true. The woman had been a pain in her ass on more than one time during her tenure with Avery Mather. Many times, she pulled her butt out of situations the girl should've never been in and maybe it was time for the young woman to get her due. Maybe this was the man to put her in her place as surely, he knew her father didn't approve of their relationship.

Leaning back, she crossed her arms over her chest yet again and a wide grin broke as she enjoyed the exchange between man and woman. If one didn't know better, Sky would swear that they were about to have sex right here in front of her. It took Jinx only a few more minutes to get the woman cuffed to himself and on the stage as she grabbed her dress to make sure it stayed in place. The roar of the crowd was deafening and Sky wished she had audio enhancements so she could hear what Angela said as Jinx danced her around the stage as her mouth moved a mile a minute.

The funniest was the moment when the man poured the ice water on her as if to drown her anger and frustration. The liquid seeped into Angela's clothes and the cold made her nipples stand at attention through the thin cotton dress. As Jinx looked at her breasts appreciatively, the girl tried to cover herself with her free hand. The next thing to happen took everyone by surprise as the moment Angela opened her mouth to make a comment to the man, Jinx swooped down and gave her a heart-stopping kiss.

Sky closed her eyes briefly and allowed the deep belly laugh to erupt before returning her gaze to the stage. She'd never laughed this hard during her time on Earth. It had been many years since humor was a part of her life.

Jinx wasn't done with the young woman as he continued to rub his now hard body against her over and over, up and down. It wasn't long before he picked her up gently, carrying her off stage left and out of view while the next number started.

Sky sat up straight. Damn, she'd lost her target. Avery wouldn't be happy at all with her for losing his daughter. The way the man carried her was incredibly tender and caused her to wonder. Sighing heavily, she frowned and narrowed her eyes. Surely, Jinx would have to bring the woman back, if for nothing except to make sure she got home to Daddy. Then again, maybe there was something she missed. Still, there was no harm with enjoying the view for a few more minutes as there was no way she couldn't track them down.

Sky looked briefly at the occupants at the table then back to the men on stage as a smile formed on her face. Looks like I'll have my night out after all, she thought smugly and turned her attention to the show on stage, hoping to get another glimpse of the two who slipped away so easy.

Chapter 2

SUDDENLY ONE DARK HAIRED man was on the table in front of her, gyrating his sexy hips in her face, his package mere inches from her mouth. In another life, she would have leaned forward and planted her lips on his crotch, willing his body to perform. She really should have been paying more attention to the situation around her instead of wondering about where Angela had gotten herself.

Leaning down, his breath reminded her of the sweetgrass that grew on her home planet of Tyrsati, heightening her senses even more. "Sweetheart, I see how you want me...it's written all over your face." His voice purred in her ear.

Sky gasped and pulled back to get a better look at the man in front of her. He reminded her of the gods of Vada. He was tall, well-muscled, dark hair brushing the top of his shoulders and had the most incredible violet eyes she had ever seen. Guess the optics weren't wrong. He would fetch an exquisite price on Texra and her mother would be extremely proud for her acquisition. She shook her head to clear the cobwebs.

"Nice eyes, sweetie – hang around after the show – I'll make it worth your while." His voice hit a resonance with her and her whole body flushed. It had been years since she had reacted to any man. Now her emotions and body betrayed her for an insignificant being on an outer planet. She shook her head. This planet was no more insignificant than any other, including her own but she knew if she didn't get herself under control, the Harvester in her would take over. Old habits die hard.

"Don't let his demeanor fool you, luvey. He just wants to get into your pants." Another deep voice reverberated close to her ear.

She glanced over her shoulder and again her breath was nearly taken away as she considered the bluest eyes she'd ever seen in the galaxy bar none. The sky of Octa couldn't hold a candle to the color that swirled in their depths.

"Ooo, Jaxon is right about the eyes. Very cool green."

"Contacts," Sky managed to get out for the second time this evening, her voice low.

"And a sexy voice to boot. Very nice." He twirled away to join his companion on stage. He was just as nice looking as the first guy but just a little shorter. His shiny hair swung around his jaw line as he moved and her hands ached to run her fingers through it and over his body.

She sat there stunned as the people at her table laughed and clapped her on the back as if she'd done some sort of fantastic feat. While her time on this planet had been very thrilling, in her old life working for her mother, their performances had to be impeccable or their fate might be worse than death. She vaguely wondered just how she'd rate them.

•••• ✷ ••••

Sky did her best to smile and act as if what happened was one of the most exciting things in her life when in reality it brought back some memories she'd rather forget. Folding her hands in front of her, she closed her eyes and steadied her breathing. She opened her eyes slow and caught a glimpse of a targeting laser. The light was in a part of the spectrum that no one of this planet could even see but her optics caught it.

Scanning the crowd, she allowed her eyes to whirl, not caring who saw. There were not supposed to be any Harvesters on this world as it had been declared too primitive to even be included in the Alliance of Planets. She came here because she knew this was the one place her mother wouldn't think to look. Now, she knew another Tyrsatian walked the same world as she did, occupying the very same room.

Maybe it was time to see just what type of trouble Angela got herself into. Leaning across the table, she quickly gave Jayne her phone number and said her goodbyes to all the others present. Rising slowly, she didn't want to alert the other Harvester but she was just far enough away and at a weird angle to not see who it might be. Moving quickly to the back wall, she moved to where she stood way behind the woman but close enough to see who it was.

Jesata Ardik. Of all the Harvesters to show up on her new home planet, one of the most relentless in the business had to land on her new home. This wasn't going to be easy. She had to delay her from marking them because once they were marked, it didn't matter wherever in the universe they were, they would be considered fugitives until captured and sold to the highest bidder. Meaning, she wouldn't be able to get them off world without the help of her mother.

Coming to stand directly behind the woman, she finally had reason to be glad of her height as she stood a few inches above the blond head. "What are you doing here?" Sky whispered close to Jesata's ear.

The surprise in her eyes couldn't be hidden as she turned to see who challenged her. "I could ask the same thing of you." The voice came out in a hiss and she swelled with the knowledge she had the upper hand as the woman turned fully in her direction.

"I asked you first." When no answer was forthcoming, she continued. "See, last time I heard this planet wasn't even on the acceptable list of acquisitions." Jesata's eyes narrowed and she knew she had her.

"How astute of you, Xera, I didn't know you even paid attention to those things. I'm sure your mother would be surprised to know someone has seen you." Her voice had a steely edge.

"I paid attention to more than you ever gave me credit for, Jesata. Leave my mother out of it. Again, I ask you, why are you here?"

The woman searched her face for a moment. "To harvest, of course, why do you think?"

Her haughty attitude rubbed Sky wrong. "That's Princess Xera to you and if this planet were up for grabs it would be mine. I found it and I claim it. Here I'm called Sky."

"Have you registered that claim?"

She wanted to slap the smug smile off the other woman's face. "I suggest you remember just who I am. You don't want to piss me off now, do you?" The drazee was pressed hard against the woman's abdomen. "After all, my mother will forgive me...but you...you're a different matter altogether."

Jesata didn't even blink an eye. "You know the law. You have one galactic week to stake your claim to this world. It will nearly take you that long to get somewhere to file your intentions."

Sky didn't show any emotion. Emotion at this point would be a weakness she could ill afford. She knew Jesata had a point. But the woman didn't know she'd installed the latest jump drive just a year ago when she took her vacation to refurbish her ship. She could make it to a drop point and be back before Jesata would be the wiser. "I know the law." She leaned in so that she touched her, nose to nose. "If you mark even one of these men, you will find yourself in a Tyrsatian prison faster than you can leap. Do I make myself clear?"

Jesata nodded. "Very. However, if I were you, I would mark those two to the left immediately. They have the right genetic makeup to be good breeders. You know how rare a male breeder is in the outer reaches."

That would explain her heightened senses. "Since when has the breeders market opened up?"

"Since a plague took all the men from Menos Prime last year. You haven't kept up on the news recently, have you?"

She wasn't about to admit anything to this woman as it had been almost nine months since she downloaded any galactic news from her ship. "It doesn't matter. Why don't you enjoy the show and just go on your merry way?"

●●●●✳●●●●

Jesata's feral smile said it all. "I hope you don't mind if I wait to see if you make the deadline. I wouldn't want to miss an opportunity."

Sky backed away slowly as the drazee slid back around her wrist and finger. "I will and your opportunities will be elsewhere." She knew she had to get back stage and quick.

Glancing around to see what her options would be, she found a door to her left and crept up the few stairs to the back of the stage. As she reached the top of the stairs, she saw Jinx and Angela in a passionate embrace. She'd nearly forgotten about them. She took a deep breath and went to stand beside them, clearing her throat.

Angela was the first to react and pulled Jinx behind her. "I recognized you at the table. What are you doing following me back here?"

The girl thought she could protect them from her. Sky closed her eyes and took a deep breath to calm her frayed nerves. "Then you know who sent me. If you don't mind me asking, just what are you doing here?"

"I love him and nothing you or my father says can stop me." A little hiccup erupted as Jinx reached out to steady her.

Sky frowned, knowing the girl had drank way too much. "Just what would I be stopping, Angela?"

"We're running away together," she stated as Jinx put his hand over her mouth.

He gave her a wry smile. "She doesn't really know what she's talking about. She gets that way sometimes."

Angela began batting his hand away. "I get that way sometimes? Are you telling me Daddy was right? All you want is my trust fund?"

"No, darling, I'm saying this woman could really hurt me and I know you don't want that to happen." He looked down at her, practically willing her to be quiet.

Sky's low chuckle felt good. "Well, that's one way of putting it." Her eyes narrowed as she scrutinized both of them. "How much you worth, Mr. McCoy?"

Surprise filtered across his face. He wasn't expecting her to question him. "As in money?"

Sky shook her head knowing she could make some wiseass comment about galactic credits. "Of course, money."

"Why? I mean, I'm not worth what her father is, if that's what you're asking." He clasped Angela's hand as she gently rubbed his arm.

"Not many men are. The problem is I believe her father doesn't think you can support her in the lifestyle she's accustomed to right now. I also believe he doesn't think you're good enough for his daughter because of this fact."

Jinx's eyes narrowed. "Not good enough. When has a Stanford graduate not been good enough?"

Sky pondered him again, knowing that Stanford was considered one of the best human schools on the planet. "So, you're educated. There are a lot of people in this country who are. You still haven't answered the money question yet."

"What difference does it make? You'll probably let him know where we are anyway." He stood there just as defiantly as Angela did.

She let out a sigh. "Look, impress me please. I've got something more pressing, which has come up, and I need to make sure Angela is going to be fine while I take care of it. Otherwise, you're right, I'll have to tell Mr. Mather where you two are. What's it going to be?"

Angela stood on tiptoe and whispered something to him making Jinx stand a little taller. "I own this revue. I make good money right now and have a million in the bank."

She nodded. It always impressed her when young men made good. It wasn't much, but it was a start. "That's a good start." Sky gave them the once over again. "I've got to check in with your father here shortly. Want me to tell him I came backstage and you were already gone?"

The young woman looked relieved. "Could you really do that for me?"

"If you promise me one thing."

Angela clutched Sky's hands. "Anything."

She looked down at the younger woman, knowing she'd never been put to the test. "You've got to promise me no more wild stunts. And you better be serious because I think this guy is probably a good man. Good men are hard to find."

Angela nodded her head, briefly closing her eyes. "I promise."

Sky scowled down at her. "You answered that one a little too fast. I mean it." She glanced at Jinx before returning her gaze to Angela. "I would be able to find you anywhere you might think you can hide. Jinx is right, I could hurt him or you if I had to do so. I'm giving you a chance to find your own way with the man of your choice. Don't make me regret my decision."

She shook her head. "No, never."

Sky looked back at Jinx. "I need you to tell me who two of your dancers are, if you don't mind."

His head bobbed up and down. "Sure. Anything for you."

"The two with the long dark hair. One has blue eyes and the other almost violet. Who are they?"

"That would be Jaxon Sinclair and Zane Nix. They're my two Scotsmen. Would you like me to introduce you to them?"

"That's not necessary. They were practically in my lap earlier." She turned to creep back off the stage before quickly turning back. "If they don't show up to work, you'll know why."

"Wow. You going to take them home with you?"

She gave the couple one more glance. "Something like that." Sky had almost made it to the stairs when the stage side door opened and her prey walked in. This would be easier than she thought.

Chapter 3

S KY STOOD AND WAITED for them, admiring their appearance even more with each step they came closer. Both were in what she knew were a type of clothing called kilts. When she first saw the plaid garment, she'd mistakenly likened them to a woman's skirt and she'd been chastised by her employer who identified with the people from a land called Scotland. Apparently, they were like a warrior clan of brave men and women. She did appreciate the ones walking toward her with their hard chests, finely chiseled abdomens, strong arms and well-muscled legs. In all her time searching the galaxy, she couldn't recall men as handsome or attractive to her and she'd seen enough men to know the difference.

She hoped they remembered their invitation and that they would forgive her in the fact it would need to be on her terms. "Hi, boys," she purred.

"Well, look who came to see us, Jaxon." Zane walked completely around her and she knew he liked what he saw as her body reflected the best she or any female could be. He fingered her dark hair and completed his circuit. "Know who she reminds me of?"

Jaxon hemmed her in on the other side and it took every ounce of her mental capacity to not throw them to the ground and hog tie them. "Who?"

She could feel that voice in her crotch and she needed to gain control. "No, don't tell me...," she gave them both a dazzling smile, "...Zena, warrior princess."

"Guess you've heard that line before." Jaxon's voice stirred emotions she thought never to have on any of the known worlds.

She could feel the soft touch of Jaxon's fingers as he brushed her hair from her neck. His velvety breath fluttered over her sensitive skin and she shuddered in anticipation. Maybe this wouldn't be as easy as she thought since the need to hog tie them was suddenly replaced with the need to fuck them. Hard and long. Closing her eyes, she knew she needed them on her ship to neutralize their effect on her. But not before she partook of the bounty placed before her while here on this world.

"I'm telling you, Jaxon, we really need to take her home tonight." Zane gave her another appreciative once over.

Well, two could play this game. "What makes you think I'll let you?"

Jaxon's throaty laugh was soft and almost as deadly as she was. "Whoa – she told you buddy."

Zane pouted a little. "You're giving us all the right signals."

It had been a while since she played the sex game. There were parts like this she missed but there were others she didn't. Strange dark things done only in dingy back rooms of places better to forget. Maybe she could draw her pleasure with the teasing game out a little longer. "Ah – come on, guys – are you going to give up that easily?"

That's all it took to get them to come close and close was all she needed. Touching her drazee which looked like a new-age bracelet-ring when not in use, she picked up two miniscule tagging devices. She smiled what she hoped was a seductive grin and tried to lure them even closer. Jaxon was the first to get close, his hard body slid along her backside, making her knees go a little weak as his hard cock pressed against her butt. Zane wasn't far behind as he came nose to nose with her, his body pressed fully into her front in a very good way. He smelled as good as he looked. She put her hand around his neck and drew him forward into a light kiss. Pressing her hand tightly against him, she pulled him closer still, her tongue gently touching his full lips.

"You taste good," she murmured before pressing her lips to his. Their tongues warred for supremacy over the other and when she pulled back she was shaken to the bone. No one had ever made her feel this way. Jaxon's hands slid around to cup her breasts and she knew if she allowed them to touch her any more, they would need to find a bed and fast. Lifting her hand, she pulled his face to her neck, feeling his tongue snake out and lick the pulse beating there.

"Jaxon...we only have a few seconds." Zane's voice cut through her mental haze.

Suddenly, the music blared and they were gone. She opened her eyes to see them going on stage apparently to perform. It didn't matter as she succeeded in successfully tagging them. Sky smiled to herself. Men everywhere were just the same. Give them a little bit of ass and they came running. Still, these two made her feel something she hadn't felt in all the years working for her mother. It was as if – no, she wouldn't let herself over think this situation. She would do what she needed to save this world then leave those two no matter how she felt.

She gave another glance toward the two performing on stage to a tune she felt appropriate as some of the words were 'Princes of the Universe.' These two could be princes somewhere but probably not in her sector of the universe. That portion was reserved for the women calling the shots and being in charge. Sky didn't know how many times she wanted to laugh when earth born would call her Xena as there were some distinct differences. The woman was way too nice in her opinion.

Sky tried to be as inconspicuous as possible going back down the stairs. She needed to get to her ship and do some prep work before she brought aboard any passengers. That was all she really expected them to be for the short time they were with her. She knew if she didn't take them with her while filing her claim, Jesata would tag them. It could take her years to get them back and by that time they would be broken or worse. She witnessed the things people did to their slaves and women were by far the worse.

Maybe it had to do with man's previous domination over females, which made the brothel owners hatred run deep of the male species. She heard some horrible things that happened to women on this planet but for the most part they were cherished and revered by the men of this world. But sometimes, men went berserk and then chaos ensued. Nothing controlled the chaos of a man's mind once he went off the deep end. If these two had the chance to explore the universe maybe they wouldn't go crazy as many on this rock had.

Sky edged back along the wall, cautious as she didn't want to see Jesata at all before she went to her ship. She needed to call Avery before she went and make some excuse. Since she had been an exemplary employee who had never called in sick once nor ever had a family emergency, she felt no qualms about asking for time off. If the man knew she planned to save their way of life, she felt sure there would be no problem but is wasn't something she could explain to him with truth.

The need to find a private place hit the top of her list as she walked around the edges of the large room. She watched the women as they responded to the two men on the stage and something in her wanted to make them stop – both the men dancing and the women oogling them. Somehow, since she tagged them they felt like hers. Not a good feeling for a Harvester to have. Harvesters were meant to hunt down their prey and deliver them to the highest bidder. In many cases that had been her mother. She'd been grateful she managed to slip away from her when she did and that was about to change. The moment she filed the paperwork to claim this planet, her mother would send a messenger with official papers. Papers which would need answers and clarification.

She really couldn't understand why some of the women of this world wanted the princess thing. Sometimes being a princess really sucked. She sighed and made her way past the bar. She had almost made it out the door when she caught Jesata close to her prey. Reaching down, she touched her drazee and clicked a button, sending out a warning signal to any other Harvester in the room. Now the woman would know she was serious, very. She didn't wait to see Jesata's reactions as she headed out the door.

The doorman stamped her hand even though she would not pass through again. She didn't need to see the men to get them on her ship. By tagging them, she'd ensured that she could snatch them at any moment through her molecular transporter. One moment they would be here and the next they would be on her ship. She needed to make sure their chamber was ready as it was easier to have new space travelers sleep their first day in space than having them ill throughout the ship while they got used to the differences between the gravity and the artificial kind generated by the ship.

Now the problem would be finding a place secluded enough to activate her ship and get her ass on it. Sky walked quickly through the area of the casino near the revue. She needed to avoid people and with this being a Friday night in Sin City, she knew it would be hard. Since her optics were already in place, she let them do what they were designed to do and one of those things was to help her find the best escape route. Finally, she found a door marked as a fire exit. Again, she touched her drazee and held it near the latch to deactivate the alarm. She looked around and unobtrusively slipped out.

Sky stood and breathed in the cool, blessed air. Many of the planets in her home system didn't have a breathable atmosphere, either by design or nature. The few which did were normally set aside for the elite and many times it had galled her that there were those who didn't share the same privileges she had. She gave the place a quick once over and noted she was totally alone. As she looked to the sky, she tapped commands on her drazee to awaken her ship. It would take almost fifteen minutes to come completely online and pick her up leaving just enough time to give Avery a call.

She frowned to herself as this was something she really didn't want to do at all. This time, instead of using the archaic cell phone, she tapped the side of her head to open her contact list within her enhanced eyes. She locked on Avery's file and started the process of dialing him. She wasn't surprised when Harold, his assistant, answered. She asked for her boss and refused to disclose the nature of her business to the man as it wasn't any of his business what job Avery had sent her on.

"Just get him, Harold. He's expecting my call," she growled in frustration. If this kept up much longer, she would have try again from the ship.

"He told me he didn't want to be disturbed," came the huffy reply.

"Listen, pip-squeak, I'll hurt you the next time I see you. I need to talk to him now." She growled again, knowing the man was gripping his throat at that very moment.

"Well, you don't have to be mean about it," he answered, then sniffed as if he were about to cry.

"Apparently, I do and you're wasting my time."

"Fine. Hold on a moment. You'll just have to listen to him rant because I disturbed him."

Sky's eyes went big and knew if she had been closer to the man, she would have already thumped him. It didn't take long for her to hear the gravelly voice of her boss with his whiney assistant's one in the background.

"You have something for me."

"I like you too, Avery."

"Sorry, dinner party that my wife set up. She's not happy Angela isn't here and now this."

She pushed her hands through her hair. "I've got some bad news."

"Umm...what do I want to hear first?"

"Neither one, sir. But I'll start with what you sent me to do."

"Hmmmf...tell me something. The suspense is killing me."

She swallowed hard. "I missed them and not by very much. Jinx and Angela disappeared back stage and by the time I got there, they were gone."

"I sent you there to get her before they got together."

She shook her head and let out a lung full of air. "Sir, I had managed to get myself at the same table. The only thing I didn't have time to study was the layout of the stage. If I had had more than a few hours' notice, I would have known all the ins and outs of the place."

"It couldn't be helped. I had just learned of her even meeting up with him tonight. I told you that."

"True, sir, but it didn't give me much time to plan. Jinx chose her as his assistant for a few of the revue's audience participation parts then took her back stage. It took me a few minutes to get back there and when I did, they were gone." She hated telling this half-truth to her boss but she wanted to give the young lovers a chance he wasn't going to give them anytime soon.

"And just how did that happen?" he barked.

"Sir, this is a show. The stage has moving parts both forward and back. Like I've stated, I didn't have a chance to check out all the escape routes prior to this show. I looked for them but they weren't anywhere to be found in the places I could look. I am sorry." She waited because at this point, it could go either way.

"I know how good your tracking abilities are...when can you start?"

"That's it, sir, I can't...at least not for a week...I've been called home for a family emergency. I'm not even sure what it is but I've been told I need to get there and file some papers. I'm afraid it's my pesky aunt hounding my sisters or something. She did say she would take the family place from them." Another half-truth and one she didn't want to think about at all.

A pause followed by a long sigh. "I don't like it but I understand. Can you at least start to track them somehow?"

Sky smiled to herself. "I can start putting out some tracers for any use of credit cards and the like, sir. I'm supposing you want me to do a complete background check on Jinx as well run the information I have on your daughter's cards."

"That would be good. Can you at least call me while you're gone? This island home of yours isn't so remote you can't do that, is it?"

You have no idea, she thought smiling to herself. "No, sir, I should be able to get you some kind of updates every couple of days. Like I said, it should only take me about a week, certainly no longer than ten days."

"Go do what you need to do, Sky Nerezsh. I expect to hear from you soon." And the line went dead. This was going better than planned.

·•••✳•••·

Chapter 4

T HE DRAZEE NOTIFIED SKY about ten seconds before
the molecular beam transported her to the main
bridge of her ship renamed Jabari Cherut. She stood still
for a moment to get her bearings before she started to
get her ship in order for travel. One of the many things
afforded her, as a princess was a sentient ship. Battle
situations were made easier if the ship could make
decisions to save everyone's life, including its own.

"Well, look who finally decided to show up." The dry
sense of humor her ship displayed grated on her already
stretched nerves.

"You knew my trips might necessitate me gone for
long periods of time." She paused, hands on hips trying
to decide what should be next. This was so not the time
for this confrontation.

"I understood that portion of your new life. I am self-
entertaining you know. What I don't understand is why
you ignored my coded priority one message."

She looked at the console confused. It's really hard
to look something in the face when it doesn't have one,
she thought wryly to herself. "What priority message? I
haven't received any communiqués from you recently.
The last was the new stream you sent me two months

ago." While Sky might not like everything about her new life on Earth, she wouldn't jeopardize the planet by ignoring priority messages.

"That explains it then. She must have been using some type of interference device."

"Who?" Now she was really confused but the pit in my stomach told her she already knew who. "Who are you talking about, Bess?"

"Elizabeth if you don't mind. I rather like the formality of my new name."

She gave a deep sigh. "Maybe I shouldn't have told you the history of the name. Explain to me just why you were sending me a coded message in the first place."

"Jesata Ardik was going to Earth, that's why."

Alarm rushed through her veins. This was not good at all as it meant her visit was deliberate. "Did her long-range scanners find you?"

"Tsk – tsk – oh ye of little faith."

"You've been watching too much Earth television again." She shook her head in dismay. Sure, Bess might be self-entertaining but the things she did for entertainment would have made mush of the normal humanoid mind.

"If the shoe fits," intoned the soothing voice.

"Quit with the clichés already." There were days when she wondered if she had been in her right mind upgrading to a sentient self-learning shipboard computer. Without a doubt, Bess had proved herself over and over. Besides, the previous iteration was sentient as well but this one seemed to go through all the stages of development. She preferred doing without the teenage stages as kids just weren't her style in this particular juncture in her life.

"If you insist."

"I do. Now tell me about Jesata. I need to know everything you have on her as she came into Earth orbit as well as the last six months before she arrived."

"This sounds serious." Suddenly, the ship was all business.

"It is serious, she wants to claim the planet." She plopped down in the Captain's chair, fingers flying over the console.

"Claim? As in harvest claim?" If a computer could sound concerned, Bess did.

Sky let out another long breath. "I know. I asserted my right of being there first and she gave me one galactic week to file all the paperwork."

"One galactic week! Are you crazy?" The tone her ship used was not lost on her.

"We can get to the Neadra Quadrant in less than a week. They have a filing station there."

If Bess could shake her head had she one, she was sure the ship would have. "That really is pushing it, Xera."

"Sky," she said through clenched teeth. "You know to call me Sky."

"For this mission, you'll need to be Princess Xera again and you know what the outcome may be."

A moment of trepidation flowed through her veins like a cold drink. There were plenty of reasons for Sky to leave her old life. "I know. Please don't remind me."

"If I don't who will?" The question asked was quite innocent yet it caused her a moment of fear.

"Thanks, Bess." Her hands continued to fly over the controls as she prepared the direct transport chamber to receive Jaxon and Zane.

"Is there something you haven't told me? It looks as if you're preparing – "

"To receive prey?" she supplied. "Trust me, Bess, it's the last thing I ever wanted to do again. But damn, Jesata was going to tag them herself if I hadn't claimed them."

"Them? As in more than one?"

Sky rubbed the back of my neck. "There are two of them, Bess."

A sound similar to a sigh erupted from the console. "Usual fare?"

It took her a moment to get the meaning as these men were in no way usual. "Earth standard should be fine."

"What do you plan to do with them once they are here?"

"Good question." She frowned and again pondered if this were the best course of action. Either way, succeed or fail, there would be consequences. "I plan to release them when the claim has been filed. I won't hold them for any reason."

"You what? They could represent a galactic year's salary! We can't afford to let them go."

She scowled at the console. "We're not hurting for money yet."

"But we will be if all you're getting is Earth currency."

Bess was correct in the fact Earth currency was only good on Earth. But Sky had known that when she chose to come to a place considered a backwater dive. Earth's inclusion into the Opsim Galactic Empire had been discussed many times but just as quickly dismissed due to their lack of sustained space travel and general technology base.

"I hear you, Bess. I think after I file this claim, I'll need to take a few freelance jobs."

"What a novel idea. I would say your chances are nil from the moment anyone finds out you are Queen Igzara's daughter."

Sighing again would not be a good thing no matter how badly Sky wanted to do so. This was turning out to be one shitty day. "Then no one can find out. We'll find something, Bess. Is their room ready yet?"

"Almost. I just need to know what type of tags you used – standard or elite?"

She swallowed hard. "Elite."

"Now I know there's something you're not telling me. Why would you waste an elite tag on them?"

"Later. Now we need to make sure they aren't performing or something." She zeroed in on their tags and pulled them up on screen. She had caught them in their dressing room or at least it seemed that way. She couldn't hear what they were saying but she could tell these two were more comfortable together than most men. Zane ran his hand over Jaxon's back in a tender stroke then leaned down and kissed the top of his head. Just seeing them together like that made her blood boil in a very sensual way.

This was going to be a nearly impossible week. "Transporting in five – four – three – two – one." She hit the button and waited to feel the additional weight in the ship.

It took less than usual to hear the pounding on the door of the room one floor down from the bridge. They would be asleep in less than five minutes but Sky needed to let them know it was she who had taken them from their home. Moving out the door, she slid down the handrails and made a right. She slowed down and wondered what she would say to them. They were the first prey she had had on this ship in over eight years. While she knew she wouldn't treat them bad, they had no such knowledge and she hoped to spare them whatever trauma she could. Sidling up to the door, she did a brief knock then stood before the portal.

"You!" yelled Jaxon as he pounded on the door. "How did we get here?"

She placed her hands on either side of the portal and leaned in. "I tagged you then transported you here. I'm sorry. I wish I had more time to explain it to you but you'll be asleep in about three minutes. This will allow you to get used to being in space."

"Space...are you fricking joking me? No one but NASA goes into space." This came from Zane who had decided a totally different approach as he stood across the room, leaning against the wall with arms crossed, watching her with cold eyes.

"Not joking and I promise I will explain everything when you wake up."

Jaxon moved like a caged animal, pacing back and forth. "It had better be good."

"Good is a relative term here." She looked from one to another and knew she was in big trouble when she finally let them out. "You really need to sit down and get comfortable. The door won't open until the sleep period is up so I can't even rearrange you should you fall."

"If you say so." Zane stifled a yawn. "We better do as she says, Jax." He slid down the back wall and sat staring at Sky. It only took a few moments for Jaxon to join him as he too slipped down the bulkhead, legs bent. In a matter of seconds, they were both out.

She hadn't noticed when looking at them in their dressing rooms they were still in kilts and Jaxon had just bared himself to her. She took a big gulp of air and stared, remembering that cock hard and pressing against her butt. She allowed her optics to spin in to get a better look and she almost immediately backed up. On Earth, the women would have said he was hung like a horse. She almost felt him sliding in and out of any orifice of her body he chose and the feeling left her weak and wanting.

Sky peeked again to see if Zane were in the same position but she wasn't as lucky the second time. She would have to wait to see what the second Scot held under his kilt. She licked her lips in anticipation because if Jaxon was any indication, Zane would look just as good and together they would fulfill many a woman's fantasy.

"If you're done drooling now, there are things you need to explain to me."

She grimaced and knew if she did any more, she'd get another lecture from the only other one who knew what she was up against. "Fine. I'm on my way." One more glance through the portal and she turned back toward the bridge. It took less than a minute to get back up the stairs and in the Captain's chair.

"You need to tell me a few things here. One is why you thought you needed to bring them here and two is why you were drooling all over the hall in front of the prey chamber."

She finalized her course for the Neadra Quadrant then leaned back in the chair. She wasn't sure if she understood it all herself. "I was sent by Avery Mather to find his daughter Angela. Apparently, she's in love with the man who owns this Knights of Fantasy male revue."

"And what does that have to do with Jesata Ardik?"

"I'm getting to that part." She gazed at the console to make sure everything was prepared for their jump window. They had another two hours at sublight speed before they could get to the nearest jump port. "I pretended to be a patron of the show."

"That must have been interesting. A Harvester looking at an all-male revue. Seemed like the place to be nine years ago."

"I know." She allowed her mind to drift back to that first year after leaving her mother's home. It had taken many months of research to figure out just where she could go and be totally away from her family. The first year she had kept in touch with her mother to keep suspicion down to a minimum and the very first time she was presented with an opportunity, she took it. "But that life is behind me now and I want to move on."

"Yet, there is prey in my hold. And not just any prey but two men who make you breathe faster, your heart beat quicker and has your skin temp spiking like you were ready for mating."

Sky cringed when she heard it put in such clinical terms. Those things could be overcome. They would have to be overcome or they would fail before they ever reached the Neadra Quad. "I'd rather not talk about it."

"Have it your way but we'll have to talk some time. Right now, you have twenty-four Earth hours to figure out your plan of attack. I still want to know exactly how all this happened and you've given me damn little to work with at the moment."

Still leaning back in her chair, she closed her eyes. Everything Bess had said was true. She would need a plan for the next galactic week to work well. "As I'm sitting there watching Angela and Jinx pussyfoot around each other for the benefit of the audience, I notice a targeting laser."

"Were your optics noticed?"

"Of course. I used the contact excuse again."

"Aren't you glad I watch all that drivel now?"

She chuckled and felt a little better. "Maybe. Anyway, I managed to slip beside the woman and found out it was Jesata."

"Did she say why she was there?"

Sky shook her head. "No, she never did. I assume she was drawn by the sexual energy."

"Strange as that wasn't what drew you here."

"You have a point." This was a troubling aspect if one thought about the situation as a whole.

"What happened next?"

"I told her the planet was mine. She told me to file the claim. Then she looked at the two in the hold in such a way it made my blood boil. So, I claimed them as well."

"Interesting. Leave anything out?"

"Not really. I caught up with Jinx and Angela in the back and told them to go on the run. I told her father I didn't see them but would track them when I got back from a family emergency. Jinx told me who these two were and then I tagged them using my usual charm. I got out of there quick after I had set the warning alarm then I brought you out of hibernation."

"I see."

Sky saw a few more console items light up. "I don't understand. Just what is it you see?"

"Don't you think it odd that not just any Harvester shows up but your old nemesis, the one who wanted to discredit you most with your mother?"

She thought for a moment and grasped the gravity of what Bess said. "I think I know where this is going."

"Really? You better because once you file that claim, we'll need to run and probably not back here for a while."

"Once the claim is made, we shouldn't have any more problems. Sure, there might be my mother to deal with and all but – "

"Sky Xera Nerezsh you can be dense sometimes. Honey, you were the prey...not the men...that woman was looking for you and she found you. Let's just hope we aren't going to find more trouble than we can handle at Neadra Quadrant."

Chapter 5

S KY SLEPT BADLY AND struggled to the drink dispenser in her room after the rest period. Thank god, she'd remembered to instruct Bess about the coffee the last time she'd been on the ship. It was one of her wicked pleasures on Earth as nothing like this even existed on Octa. The rich aroma filled the air and she felt better just breathing it in.

She glanced down at her drazee to check the time. She had about two hours before her captives woke up and she needed to be her best. She took a deep breath and decided to do a little of another Earth learned trait, yoga, which was a lot like yetza on her home world. The exercise taught her how to focus better and really zero in on what needed to be done during the course of a long day. She wanted to be a calm and assertive person when talking to Jaxon and Zane.

"Well, I guess I don't have to tell you to rise and shine."

She grumbled back. "No, you don't. Is there something you need? Otherwise I should really be getting ready for the day."

"I just wanted to remind you that your men will be waking up in approximately two hours."

"I know. I need to exercise then get in the shower if you don't mind."

"You sure are grumpy without your coffee any more. What's wrong with you?"

What was wrong with her? Never in her life had she been compelled to claim a planet as her own. She had found plenty of them and never claimed any of those backwater worlds. But this one – Earth – this one was different. "Like you said, I haven't had my coffee if you don't mind." She practically growled at Bess.

"Fine. Do your exercise, have your coffee. I'll just let them out when they wake up."

"Bess – what do you want from me?"

"I want to know why I have prey in my hold. I want to know why suddenly we're on a mission to claim a planet you shouldn't care a whit about."

Back to the whys. She sighed again and leaned against the table, cup in hand. "I can't explain why, Bess. I just feel it's the right thing to do."

"Now, we're getting somewhere."

Sky frowned. "Getting somewhere? What do you mean by that?"

"Answer a few more questions and I'll give you my diagnosis."

"Look, you're not a natara and you know it."

"It's been a while since I heard that word."

"And it will be a while before you hear it again." She rubbed her forehead. "We don't live in the same world we did, Bess. You know it, I know it."

"True, but we'll be going back to our old world and we need to hone up on some things that kept us alive all those years."

Bess was right as usual. This wasn't going to be an easy task since she would be moving backwards to a place she'd rather not be at all. "There is some merit to what you're saying. I need to be able to think first before I can get a plan together. Would you at least give me some time to think?"

"This whole thing has you a little more than upset, doesn't it?" The computer's quiet, soothing tone washed over her. If it were a person, she would curl up in her lap and tell the machine all her troubles but she'd never ever been afforded that luxury as a child, why would she have it now.

"I might be a little more upset than usual, Bess."

"Could it be because I figured out you were the prey?"

She took another sip of her coffee. "That's part of it. I mean how could I just not pick up on the fact she just wasn't watching the men."

"Easy. Your guard is down because you haven't had to watch your back in eight years."

"My guard should never be down." Her voice sounded a little gruff to her own ears and hoped the computer would just ignore the implication.

"As much as you tried to hide your tone, I'll ignore it for now. It's true your guard should never be down. But this world, for all its beauty, is a technological nobody in the big picture."

"My point exactly. How could someone track me here when I left no trail?" Sky sat the cup on her bedside table and pulled her mat from its storage place. She placed it in the center of the room and started her stretching routine.

"I'm thinking it was just a shot in the dark. We are on the very outer edge of the Opsim Galactic Empire's reach. It was only a matter of time before the outer worlds started being explored."

Going down in a dolphin pose, Sky could feel the muscles in her legs and shoulders stretch. It was a good yet hard opening move but one which released up all the mental pathways. From there she went into a downward dog, held it for a few moments and slowly went back to standing. She went down into a crane pose before seating herself on the floor to finish her routine. The whole thing took her about twenty minutes and at the end her revitalization was complete. She took in a couple of deep cleansing breathes and reached for her coffee.

"Jesata said something about all the men dying out on Menos Prime. Could you check into that for me? I don't want any harm done to Jaxon and Zane because I decided to take them with me. If there is some kind of plague, we may need to avoid people from that area."

"From what you've said, it's not like you had any other choice."

"I didn't. Jesata would have tagged them herself."

"Even if your mark was on them?"

She nodded. "She would."

"Pretty bold, don't you think?"

"It wouldn't be the first time the woman has been caught poaching before. I can't say I expected her to stop because of who I am."

"She should...your mother..." Bess's voice trailed off as if she just realized what she said and to whom she was saying it.

"My mother may be powerful and wouldn't hesitate a moment to take a life. I'll admit, when the situation warrants such an action, I'm not above doing the same. But...Jesata likes it...she gets pleasure out of torturing things. Perverse pleasure." Sky shuddered when she thought about it. This was something she could not do even under the worst circumstances. It was one of the reasons she had to leave as many firstborns in her line had taken the heads of their mothers to claim the throne. In some instances, it was expected. She didn't want to wait around to find out.

"Don't get all mushy on me now."

Brought out of her thoughts, she shook her head. "I'm not getting mushy."

"Earth has made you soft. Maybe you can use those men for something more than eye candy."

She bristled at the thought. "What did you have in mind? Not that I really want to know. I'm just curious."

"Sparing is a good thing. When was the last time you had a good fight?"

Sky carried that question into the shower with her, she tried to remember when she had a match that wasn't planned and choreographed. As hard as she tried, she couldn't remember the last time she actually had someone come at her in an out and out combat situation. She stood under the cool water and thought about just how many times she had been in a fight with another humanoid. She had had a number of occasions where those she battled weren't even in the same species chain. Those were scary now that she thought about it. She shuddered to think about the eight-armed thing on

••• ✳ •••

Gectos Minima. There was something to be said for the Earth saying happy thoughts, she mused.

The system finished with warm streams of air to dry her body. Standing in front of the mirror, she appreciated the fact her shape was pleasing to the human eye. Still she wondered just what it was that drew her to them like a moth to a flame or in her world a gianta tu pyros. She had no answers and she wasn't sure today would provide anything more than an unquenchable thirst for anything but hard sex. Yeah, that one would keep her going for a long time. A galactic week was approximately ten working Earth days when comparing the two. Ten days to be completely alone with two of the most handsome men she had ever seen. She wanted to touch herself to end the ache but there was no fun in that at all.

She let out a long slow breath and walked out into the main room. She pulled out a drawer and found an old, faded pair of Earth jeans. They were comfortable and familiar and she had been looking for them for months. Pulling them on, she found a black t-shirt top and some slip-on shoes. Going out to the bridge, she knew she would need to check on how their trip went before wandering down to the prey-holding tank.

Sky went to the bridge and sat down at the main console. Her eyes quickly scanned all the most important gauges before going to the news feeds Bess had pulled up for her. Jesata was correct in saying most of the men had died out on Menos Prime. A pathogen of unknown origin was supposedly to blame but no firm answer had been coming from the ruling class. The population ran scared as was evident in the vids she watched. Children were crying for dead fathers and women were mourning their mate but no one had a reason for it to happen. On the other hand, she could think of one or two.

"Bess, this news vid is a couple of weeks old. Can you pull up anything more recent?"

"That's just it...there isn't anything."

"Don't you think that's a little odd? I mean all their men died...wouldn't they have put out a call for Harvesters?"

"It's possible. You knew that Menos was in the process of becoming an equal society...right?"

She sat there for a moment. That was almost never heard of in her part of the world. Women didn't share power, not even with their mates. "Why would they do that?" she asked confused.

"The population of men was dwindling even before their plague. It's my understanding that in order to appease the men and not stress them out, you know men can't be breeders under stressful conditions, the rulers decided to make them their equals."

"I'm sorry but that is unbelievable. You and I know anyone related to my mother wouldn't give up their power."

"Ah...that's right...the Queen Arika was a cousin or something to Queen Igzara. How many generations back?"

"I don't know...I just know they're related back there somewhere...why?"

"It might be a piece of useful information. You never know."

"Whatever you say. How long until the men wake up?"

"About ten minutes. Are you ready for them?"

Sky took a deep breath and thought about the situation. If she told Bess she wasn't ready for them to be awake, she wasn't sure what the ship would do. She knew if she claimed to be ready, Bess would expect her to take them in hand immediately and show them the ropes. To be honest, she didn't even know if she could be in the same room with them without wanting to bed them. At the same time. It scared her more than any battle she had ever been in during the entire time she was a Harvester. That life seemed like eons ago but some memories died hard.

It had never been an easy life. Most prey didn't want to be caught while some were ready to be owned and dominated by a woman, any woman. The men in her mother's brothels were treated fairly and with the utmost respect. Her mother always made it a show of giving them a choice. Little did they know the other choice was a work detail in some of the worse places in the galaxy. By the time they understood their mistake, it was too late. Another reason for her to leave. Everyone deserved to be the master of his or her own fate.

"Yoohoo...seven minutes now...what were you thinking about? Your navel?"

Sky stared at the console. She really hoped this teenage phase would be over soon. "Navel sounds good."

"Look, they are starting to move around. I suggest you take in one of your sticks."

"No." The stick Bess referred to was similar to a shock collar or a cattle prod on Earth. It was a

・・・● ✳ ●・・・

humiliating thing to do to another humanoid and she refused to even think about it. "These are not like some of the wild men we've run across, Bess. These men are educated and in most cases completely docile."

"Have it your way. Should I be on standby?"

"Just monitor the situation. You'll know if I'm in any danger."

"Will there be a knockdown, drag out?"

She gave a chuckle. This time the Earth saying actually fit one possible circumstance. "There might be." She jumped up and headed for the door. "I'm on my way. Leave us alone unless you hear me screaming for you…is that clear?"

"Very, Captain."

She swallowed hard and went down a level to stand before the holding tank. "Can I go in yet, Bess?"

"The lock opened about three minutes ago."

"Thanks. Remember what I said."

"Will do. Good luck."

"I'll need it."

She open the door and peeked inside. The men were still up against the bulkhead but curled around each other apparently for warmth. Sky went to stand over them, taking in just how they looked after a forced sleep. Some men were absolutely horrible after being shoved into a cell then woken up somewhere along the way. Not these two. Jaxon and Zane were as handsome now as they were the moment she first saw them.

Hunkering down, she allowed a hand to wander over Jax's hair. She wanted to pushed her fingers through to the back of his head and pull his full lips to her own. She turned to Zane and ran her hand over his hard biceps.

Her breath hitched a moment and she wondered again just why these two affected her so much. More than that, she knew she wanted more than just sex as something knotted her deep inside where these two were concerned.

She licked her lips in anticipation of what might happen, of what she wanted to happen. They had been in their dressing room when she took them, so both had light robes on over their kilts. She pushed the fabric out of the way and ran her fingers down Jax's firm abdomen. He had a very light smattering of hair, not quite noticeable whereas Zane was hairless but his body was just as muscular.

Boldness took hold of Sky and she wanted to touch them more, to fondle their packages just as if she had been a real Harvester again. Part of the job was to insure everything was in proper order. Sliding her hand down Jax's front, she moved her hand under his kilt and a moan of pleasure rewarded her. She moved closer and felt the weight of his penis in her hand. It would be more than adequate in size once fully excited.

The man turned over and arched his cock toward her just a little. Sky moved her thumb across the tip and felt the organ jump a little. Wait a minute...she had barely enough time to get the words out in her mind when she found herself flat on her back as violet eyes moved over her.

"I want to know just what the hell game you're playing."

She stared at him a moment and stayed completely still. "No game."

"Lady, you should have a better explanation than that one."

She felt another set of hands on her body and she creamed herself in anticipation as they continued up her body.

"Jax...let's just do her right now...screw the explanation."

··•• ✳ •••·

Chapter 6

Sky immediately understood this was an explosive set of circumstances. She sensed her explanation, though needed, would give her little lead way but she also knew she would have had trouble in the same situation. She gazed into Jax's beautiful eyes and remained still, his cock twitching. "You could just ask, you know."

As if realizing what he had done, he pushed away from her. "No. We need to see where she's really taken us, Zane."

The hands caressing her legs stopped. "You mean we can't fuck her?"

Jax's wry chuckle reverberated in the room. "I didn't say that at all. We just need some answers."

He moved his upper body away from her using the strength of his arms alone to leverage himself up. She did her best to try not to show either one of them just how interested she was. If they looked close, they would notice she failed miserably. "Thank you."

Jax stayed between her legs and looked down at her. "You might not thank us later at all."

A slow smile curved her lips. "Really?" Sky licked her lips. "Have you looked around to see where you are? Did you even realize your molecules were pulled apart during transport? Or that it was my computer who had the technology to put them back together again?" Their look of disbelief didn't stop her little tirade. "You are on my ship. My ship. Not some derelict Harvester whose hold could kill you just by breathing its air. You are on a first-class ship with first class accommodations and weapons. I treat my captives well but I'd be a little careful if I were you."

Zane jumped up and looked down them. "I hear what you're saying lady, the trouble is I don't understand a word of it." He walked to the portal and looked outside. "I can't see a thing."

Sky rolled her eyes. "That's because we're in jump space, you moron."

"Hey, that's no reason to call people names. We're not even close to being morons." Jax frowned at her and went to stand by the window as well before turning back. "Jump space as in hyperdrive?"

She swallowed hard and stood. "As in hyperdrive. If you promise to behave, you both can come to the bridge with me."

Zane quirked his eyebrow. "And if we don't?"

"My ship might just choose to kill you." She got up and walked out the door. She hated being bitchy but if she wasn't, she would be leading them to her bedroom instead of the bridge. She needed them to understand where they were and the problem at hand before sex could enter the equation. She had creamed herself in obvious anticipation when Jax's body was on hers and heaven help her, when Zane's hands had reached her inner thighs all she wanted to do was rip off their clothes and bump pelvises big time.

She climbed the steps but realized quick they weren't on her heels. She stuck her head back down. "Are you two coming or what? Please don't tell me I need to lock you back into the hold because I won't like doing that."

When they arrived on the bridge, Sky was in the Captain's chair with her legs curled under her. At this point of the trip, the stars looked like pinpoints of smeared light. She looked down again at the various instruments and noted the inverter had a slight spike in the reading. "Bess, can you check the inverter? We have a spike and I don't want to drop out of the jump because there's a problem with the ship."

"I'd rather stay right here if you don't mind." The ship practically purred.

"Nothing is going to happen." Her lips went into a tight line and she turned to the men standing in awe behind her. "Will it, boys?"

"Who is speaking? I thought you said it was just us." Jaxon gave her an accusatory stare.

She rolled her eyes. "Elizabeth is a sentient ship. I call her Bess because she loves the stories of Elizabeth the first when she was a girl."

Confusion spread across Zane's face. "A sentient ship? Are you kidding me?"

She shook her head. "No...but sometimes I wish I was."

"I heard that...you could hurt my feelings you know."

Sky rolled her eyes. "Yes, Bess, could you please check on the inverter now?"

"Hmmf. Fine. I get it you want to talk without me being here. Tell me when I can come back into the room." Her meaning wasn't lost on Sky, who merely frowned.

"Sorry. I upgraded her about a year ago, but I spent most of my time on Earth immediately after. The upgrades are meant to be done when a lot of people or at least one is around so the computer learns from interactions with those around it."

Jax gazed at the console area before leaning back. "Where were you?"

She stared at them for a few moments before deciding she would have to tell them damn near everything for them to understand what happened. "I work for Avery Mather."

"The Avery Mather?" A hint of excitement could be heard in Zane's voice.

Sky turned toward him. "I take it you know him."

"The whole city knows him. He's the homeboy made good and just about owns the town." The excited look, which crossed Zane's face, wasn't lost upon her. She had seen it many times in the course of her work.

"That's what I hear. Anyway, work's been busy these last few months and I haven't gotten back to my ship as much as I should have." She looked the men up and down. "Otherwise, I would have known Jesata was in the vicinity."

A perplexed expression crossed Jax's face. "Jesata?"

She let out a huge sigh. If she explained Jesata, she would have to explain every little detail about her life. "Might as well pull up a chair and I'll explain it to you both." She pressed a button on the console and two more chairs rose from the floor. "Then I never want to discuss it again. Is that clear?"

Zane plopped down and held up his hands. "You have the obvious advantage here, lady. I would say we are at your mercy."

She closed her eyes slowly as similar words had been used the last time she had taken prey. It was nearly enough to make her stomach turn. "Please, don't say that,' she whispered in a husky voice. "I'm sorry I took you but it truly was for your own protection."

Jaxon sat down more slowly. "You sound as if that pains you in some way."

Sky raised her eyes up to his. "You have no idea."

"Why don't you explain it to us?" Jax watched her carefully, his eyes never averting from her face.

She nodded once. "As you can see from this star map, we are no longer in the vicinity of Earth." She pointed to a screen, which held something akin to the tracking shown on cross-ocean flights. Earth could be seen a fair distance in the opposite direction. "While I was at the show tonight I saw a woman, who does what I used to do."

"And just what is that? Besides being something to Avery Mather." Jaxon leaned back in his chair and crossed his arms.

She chewed on her lip for a moment. Just being near them screwed with her mind as all she wanted to do was bed them. "I am what is known as a Harvester."

"A Harvester?" Zane leaned forward, his hands folded in front of him. "Just what does a Harvester do?"

"In my case, I harvested men for my mother's brothels as well as any planet who paid top dollar." She couldn't raise her eyes to look at them.

"You took people?" Jaxon's voice boomed in the small space.

Sky looked up and suddenly felt very small. "I took men. Most of them were living a horrible existence where they were and I offered them a better life. Or at least I thought I was in most cases."

"What kind of society needs to harvest men?"

She turned to Zane and looked at him carefully. "One who doesn't have a readily available supply. Where I come from we live in a matriarchal society in which only women are in charge."

"Then what role does a man play?"

She arched her brow at Jax. "Other than sex toy you mean?" Sky waited for his nod before continuing. "Not very much. Men have no dealings with the way things are run in any manner. There does appear to be a planet or two where the women want to share power but I'm sure an uprising would have happened there until the plague which killed off all their men."

Jax crossed his arms. "How can you be so certain? And what is it about this plague?"

She gave him a sideways smile. She liked his no nonsense type of personality and couldn't wait to learn more about him. "Over the years, there was never a successful integration of men and women in any place where power had to be shared. The few times there were, the ruling body, which suggested equality, were assassinated first then questions asked. The planet which most recently suggested that is where the plague just wiped out the men."

"Will the plague affect us if we go there?" Zane's look of concerned mirrored her thoughts.

"I don't have a clue but that isn't where we need to go."

"Just where is this mysterious place and why do we need to go there?" The fierce look on Jax's face did little to calm her already frayed nerves.

"We have to go to the Neadra Quadrant so I can file a claim for this planet."

"What type of claim? And why would you have to claim something you don't own?"

She expelled the air in her lungs as a raspy gasp. "It's complicated."

"Uncomplicate it for us, sweetheart." Zane sat back in his chair.

She looked at Jaxon once before starting. "This might get boring or be to technological. Ask questions when they arise please. Like I said before, I don't want to have to repeat myself more than once. Is that clear?"

"Perfectly."

"Absolutely, sweetheart."

Her gaze took in their handsomeness once more and knew the moment she finished, she would be lost. "Would you like something to drink before we start? It's going to take a while."

"What do you have, doll?" Zane's smile melted her resolve a smidgen.

"I have anything you might find on Earth in most cases. I have soda, coffee, even tea if that's what you'd like."

"A cup of tea would be nice. Do you have water?"

"Of course. Jaxon? Anything?"

"Water," was his terse reply.

She got up and went to the food replicator to key in their requests. "This is the main food and drink replicator on the ship. There's another in the galley, one in my room and one in each of the three main guest quarters. The language is Tyrsatian. This presents another problem in itself, as we'll need to get you universal translators. They are installed right behind your ear under your skin and are nearly invisible. It will enable you to read and speak any language you encounter. It will help keep you safe for the most part. Of course, it won't help with the societal nuances within a society. Those are only picked up with time. I'm hoping your time on this ship and traveling the universe will be limited."

Sky quickly programmed the machine to produce the requested drinks. Taking the hot tea out of the dispenser, she carried it to Zane. "Do you need anything for it?"

"Sugar is always good and a little cream if possible would be nice."

"Not a problem." Going back to the dispenser, she clicked a few buttons and another door right next to the main popped open. Inside were a variety of stirring utensils as well as packets of sugar and a variety of creamers. "I hope you don't mind this kind right now. I'll need to make sure that Bess has the replicator programmed correctly for dairy products. I wouldn't want to give you something you can't eat or worse yet, might kill you."

"Nice to know, luv." Zane took the tray he was offered.

She turned back and again programmed the machine to put out a huge glass of water. "This is equivalent to your bottled water on Earth. Let me know about the taste. Like I said, I haven't had Bess check a lot of things yet but we'll need to do so quickly."

Taking the glass from her, Jaxon glared for a moment before taking a long drink. "It's passable."

She gave him a wry smile before returning to the Captain's chair. After a brief glance at the console, she turned back to them. "Getting back to the problem at hand."

"I want to know why you took us." Jaxon stared at her with hard eyes.

"I don't know if you noticed another woman there. She was tall like me and looked different."

Zane took a sip of the warm liquid. "I do recall seeing another woman I would categorize as an Amazon...just like you, honey."

She smiled to herself. This one was going to be easy to convince of her true nature. "Believe me when I say, she is nothing like me."

"Then why don't you tell us what she's like."

She understood Jaxon's resentment of the situation but it was something she couldn't change in the least. "Cruel. She would just as soon see you send to the mines of Treygar as anything else. She also wouldn't hesitate to starve you should you not live up to her expectations. And in the worst-case scenario, you could expect her to torture you because that's what turns her on."

"Torture? As in blood and guts type of torture?"

Sky shook her head. "Hers would be of a more sexual nature designed to make sure you never have pleasure again with anyone, male or female."

Jaxon blanched a little at that. "You say this woman was there at the show?"

She nodded again. "She was there at the show and the only reason I tagged you then took you with me. She's stolen prey from me before and then I would find out much later they arrived at their destination dead."

"Is that what could have happened to us?" Zane's very serious look tugged at her heartstrings.

"With my dying breath, I would never let that happen. I don't kill people unless they are trying to kill me. And never for pleasure. There are better ways to get what I want from someone." She stared at them long and hard, willing them to get her meaning.

Jaxon narrowed his eyes. "We won't be your sex slaves. Is that why you brought us here?"

"I'm not sure just why I brought you here at all. I just know..." she hesitated knowing the moment she revealed this they would be equals, "...you two turn me on like no others ever have done."

Chapter 7

A WIDE GRIN BROKE OUT on Zane's face. "Did you hear that, Jax? We turn her on. I told you there was something there."

Jaxon turned to look at the man with a stark look. "I never said we didn't turn her on. That much was evident when we kissed her back stage. What I want to know is what she wants from us now."

Sky had failed miserably in giving the details accurately and those would be the only thing that saved them. It had been so long since she'd done anything for anyone except Avery Mather. Her dealing with him had been smooth and efficient. She'd forgotten just what it meant to deal with living, breathing, emotional humanoids. "Look, the bottom line is I didn't want you killed."

A look of concern flashed across Jaxon's handsome face. "You think she would have killed us."

"I really don't know. I just know that Bess thinks she was after me and not you two. By forcing me to claim the planet, she now has me in her territory."

"And your old haunt if what I'm hearing is correct."

She nodded. "Yes, I'm an alien from a planet called Tyrsati."

"Wow…a real live alien…are the other women from your planet as hot as you?"

Jax gave Zane a frustrated look. "Can't you tell for once this isn't fun and games here? This seems to be some serious shit and we need to know all we can."

A new respect for the man flooded her being. He was practical and handsome, a rare combination where she came from. "Jaxon's correct. We need to figure out just what is happen before anything else. If Bess is correct, I've dragged you into an even bigger mess."

"Can't we have sex first then worry about the details later?"

Both Jaxon and Sky turned to give him a withering look before they looked at each other and laughed. "Is he always like this?"

Jaxon shook his head. "No, I think you scared him good and he's compensating by being the funny man."

"Not fair telling all my secrets." Zane lifted a pinky and took another sip of tea.

Jaxon's warm chuckle boomed in the small space. "No one knows all your secrets."

"True. Still, they aren't yours to tell."

Sky felt like a third wheel as the two of them tossed their easy banter about. She tried to relax and realized she couldn't. She wanted them with every fiber of her being. She had never had any men, prey or otherwise, make her feel this way. "The secrets can wait as can the banter. We need to devise a plan. Do either of you have any battle training?"

"Whoa, this is going way beyond fun here. Why would we need to have fighting skills?" Jaxon turned back to her with a very serious expression.

Her heart sank. Maybe she had seriously misjudged them. Maybe their bodies were all for show. "I just thought – "

Suddenly, Jaxon knelt on the floor in front of her. "I didn't say we had no skills. I'm asking why we would need them." His voice was soft like a breeze all warm and sexy on a summer's day. His closeness brought her new sensations and all she wanted to do was reach out to caress his face. Yet she hesitated.

"I'm afraid I've done you a bigger disservice than just taking you from your home." She swallowed hard and looked down at her hands. Why was she having such difficulty? What was wrong with her? She was strong in both mind and will but here she acted like little a girl who had no knowledge of the word sex. She had always considered herself hard and these two had her all soft.

His hand touched the side of her face and she leaned into it. "Explain it to me, Sky. I need to know what we're up against."

His eyes were limpid pools of violet not unlike some of the private ponds on her family's estate on Tyrsati. "If it's true that I was Jesata's prey, then I'm afraid there is some sort of family feud going on."

His hand buried itself in her hair. "What type of feud?"

"The murder kind." She sighed and rubbed her cheek against his palm, letting her tongue flick out and give it a light brush. "In our society, it's not infrequent for the oldest daughter to kill the mother to gain the throne. I left because I didn't want to kill my mother. I care for her deeply and our house isn't run in the same manner as most."

"And just how is it run, lass?" Zane placed gentle hands on her shoulders and began kneading them as if to ease the tension.

"My mother is fairer than most in my world. Most prey brought in live very luxurious lives within our brothels."

"How can being a slave be considered luxurious?" Zane's lilt flowed through her, tingling her very soul.

"Believe me it's better than most conditions for men." She rotated her neck slow and easy, allowing his fingers to slide over her clothes. Sky never knew one could have such feelings with one's clothes on. "Most men live on primitive planets or have been captured for tenure in the mines. It doesn't matter which one as all of them are the same."

"Why have we sunk to such a low position?"

Jaxon's breathe fluttered across her face and she turned to look at him, noting he was mere inches away. "Millennia ago, men ruled our galaxy. We had years of wars and everything, which come with them. We were almost wiped out as the men became greedier wanting more and more. Finally, one of my ancestors said it was enough and the women rose against them. At first, it wasn't much of a battle but soon we became the dominate sex, slowly taking over governments and elite houses. Once we had the power, we made sure war would never be waged on such a large scale."

"So, the houses battle?"

Sky nodded. "Mainly. Sometimes we battle for territory, sometimes rights to certain men. It's almost never the same as we all have accumulated wealth and power over the years. None of us need anything. This along with the fact I didn't want to kill my mother to gain her power made me leave my home. No one had ever explored the outer universe's rim worlds, so I disappeared amongst them to live out my life."

"And now?" Jaxon leaned in and placed a feathery kiss on her cheek. "How do you feel about that life?"

She closed her eyes and enjoyed the awareness they brought to her. She had been alone for a long time. She didn't want to be alone any more. She bent forward and placed her hands on his shoulders. "I don't want to be alone anymore," her voice a rough whisper. Her lips grazed his and she knew immediately she wanted more.

Jaxon's hands slid around her abdomen and pulled her close while another set of hands cupped her breast through her thin cotton t-shirt. Taking his face in her fingers, she gazed deeply into his eyes. "I don't know why but you two are special."

"Of course, we're special, sweetheart, otherwise you wouldn't have picked us. Don't you agree, Jax?"

"Absolutely."

She loved the way his mouth moved, his lips all full and tempting. She pulled him to her and tried to devour his lower lip. He tasted like the honey from the canta bees at home, all tangy with just a hint of sweet. Slipping her tongue in his mouth, her surprise continued as she savored him when his tongue rose to war with hers. Most men she'd known were timid and meek whereas this one would take what he wanted not just what she was willing to give.

Zane's hands slipped inside her shirt and cupped her breasts. "Don't forget about me, lass." His tongue was warm on her ear and she gasped. She pulled her mouth from Jaxon and turned to him, giving him a hard kiss. He tasted just as good and she was truly at a loss, as she wanted both of them at once. This astounded her, as she had never had two men at the same time. Nevertheless, she needed them, desired them in a way, which made her burn inside. She almost came undone when she felt a mouth on her breast. She should take them back to her quarters but there was something wicked about making out on the bridge of her ship.

"Should we be doing this here?"

The voice sliced through her sex-filled daze as she turned to look back at Jaxon. "What? I can't believe you're asking me that now. I hoped to initiate the bridge." Desire, low and sexy edged her voice.

"The chair seems kind of tight for three," Zane said as he continued his assault on her neck.

"You haven't seen anything." Sky freed a hand and pressed a few buttons on the arm. The chair reconfigured itself to accommodate all of them with no back at all. "This ship is the top of the line in luxury. Prey is meant to be tested on the long journey to where they are going."

"Do all Harvester's test the merchandise?"

"It depends upon the Harvester. I've tested my share."

Jaxon watched her for a few moments, his hand never stopping his movements. "Have you ever had two men, lass?"

She looked at them through hooded eyes. "Never," she whispered.

"Then you're in for a treat." He reached for her jeans and started undoing the buttons. "Take her shirt off, Zane. You start there and I'll start here."

"Why do you always get the fun?"

Jaxon stared at her for a moment. "I'm hoping this won't be just a onetime thing. Am I wrong?"

She shook her head. "I can't imagine once will be enough."

He looked up at Zane. "See, you'll get your turn."

"Fine. Lift your arms." Zane stripped her shirt off her in one fluid motion.

He sat next her to and leaned over to take her nipple into his mouth, rolling it with his tongue. She moaned as the experience tugged at her core, making her crotch tingle in anticipation. Jaxon had finished with her jeans and tugged them down her legs, planting gentle kisses along her inner thigh as he moved them out of the way. She glanced down and saw him stare at her body for a moment before moving his mouth to her.

His tongue licked her from bottom to top, never touching her clit. She arched and tried to bring that part of her body into contact with him but she couldn't as he'd moved just out of her reach. She felt him spread her labia even more and his fingers stroked her leaving her to shudder with desire. She wouldn't last long if he kept this up and she needed more. His fingers slid inside her while his thumb and tongue continued its work on her clit.

"I'm going to slide my finger in your ass. If you've never been fucked there, push down when I first enter you."

She had engaged in anal play and looked forward to the thrill it would give her. In short order, she had a finger in her ass and one in her vagina with the pleasure surrounding her in a tight grip. Soon she was a piece of quivering flesh as Jaxon began to move his fingers in and out of her quickly. He used his tongue to stroke her again and she almost lost it. She wanted them both in her when she orgasmed but the man seemed intent on bringing her to the crest then bringing her back down. Her pussy throbbed in expectation of their next move.

"Hey, I want some of that," Zane murmured and leaned in to get a quick kiss from Jaxon. There was something very sensual when she watched them kiss, not unlike what she saw on the monitor earlier. It quickened her pulse and made her pussy clench even more. "You taste like the sweetest cream ever." He inclined himself forward until he was a breath away from her. "See for yourself, sweetheart."

His mouth consumed hers as she tasted herself on him. No man had ever done that to her and it was interesting they knew just how to turn her on more. Maybe there was something to be said for free men. Free men took what they wanted it seemed and she would be the better for it.

"I want you in me now," she murmured hoarsely.

"Anything for you, lass." Jaxon took one final sweep with his tongue. "I'll be on the bottom, Zane. Be gentle...I can tell it's been a while for her."

He swooped her up in his arms and laid back on the couch, every inch of their skin touching as he put her on top. She didn't even become conscious of the fact they had shucked their robes and kilts. She ran her fingers up his smooth chest and saw his eyes darken in response.

"You want to climb on or do you want to do it yourself?"

She was suddenly aware of his hard shaft sliding along her crack. She glanced back and her earlier touch hadn't even aroused him because he was huge. And huge was what she needed. "I'll get on."

Straddling him, her leisurely descent allowed her to accommodate not only his girth but his length as well. Breathing heavily, she moved her hips from side to side to fully seat herself on him. He rubbed against her inner spot and she knew just a few thrusts would put her over the edge. Jaxon reached up and grabbed her tits, massaging them into tight peaks. She moaned in pleasure and again shuffled against him to feel him rub her inside.

"We can't forget, Zane," Jaxon admonished lightly.

She turned and saw he had his hand on himself, making himself even harder. Stretching out her hand toward him, she motioned for him to come forward. "Please – please – I want both of you," she said in a breathless whisper.

He nodded once, took position behind her, pushing her forward, and ran his hand where Jax and Sky were joined. He pulled the wetness from their bodies and ran his fingers over her tight rosette. "Tell me you've had anal sex. I don't know how controlled I can be as you two have me really turned on." His breathing was strained as well.

"Yes, just never two men at once" she replied with a ragged breath, moving her ass as his fingers played with her.

"Good." He took position behind her and thrust into her body with a solid stoke. His groan of pleasure filled the space. "You are so tight."

Her breaths came short and sweet. "And you two fill me like no one has ever done before."

Jaxon brought them back to reality. "I need to move or it will be over before it even starts."

He moved slow, skin against skin, sliding in and out of her as Zane did the same. Wave after wave of pleasure washed over her with each stroke, each movement. Her body was on fire as they all murmured their assent to the lovemaking. She barely recognized Jaxon's command as the groans reached a near crescendo.

"Go slower, Zane, I want her to come with us."

"I'll try, mate," he moaned, "I'm not sure I can make it."

The pace became more deliberate as they pulled her closer to a total meltdown. "Yeah – please – yes – fuck me. Harder. Please." Each word was pulled from her very soul as they moved in and out of her body.

They seemed to linger over each stroke, one in, one out, as they plummeted her toward completion. The sensations swelled into a crescendo and without warning sparked a super nova, shattering her into a million pieces like a star into the heavens. She cried out her release as the feelings continued to build, pushing her more than ever. Soon their cries joined hers as the fire consumed them all in a molten haze of pleasure.

Chapter 8

SKY LAY ON TOP of Jaxon, her fingers lightly skimming the flesh on his abdomen, her leg over his. Zane snuggled her backside as the bliss fulfilled her in total completion. She'd never thought she would feel this way. There were women on Tyrsati who had never found their soul mate and here she had found not one but two on a primitive, rim world. Unexpectedly, she could understand why women wanted to share the power with a man or men such as she had found.

She closed her eyes and let out a big sigh. This would not go over well with her mother who had never achieved bliss in all her years, each child by a different father as she looked for her mate. Sky knew that wasn't quite true because she felt certain if her father had lived, they would still be together. Mother had always talked with such devotion whenever he was mentioned.

"What are you thinking?"

Jaxon's voice carried a soothing quality that she needed at the moment. She was not prepared to let them know just what they meant to her. Not yet. Knowledge was power and she couldn't afford them to fall into the wrong hands, as they would surely be used against her. "I'm not really thinking anything," she murmured.

"Och." Zane's chuckle tickled her back. "She told you, friend."

She snickered as well. "That's not what I meant. If it's any consolation, my mind is free of thought except of you two."

"I suppose if we're not careful you'll be telling us we complete you."

It was everything she could do to keep caressing Jaxon's chest. If she faltered, he would surely know how she already felt about them. She needed to analyze those feelings so she could deconstruct them and find out how they got under her skin so very, very quickly. It had only been two earth days since she had first seen them. A mere forty-eight hours and here she was, naked on her bridge intimately entwined with two handsome men who she cared about. "That sounds like it's something from a movie," she quipped.

"Probably, lass. He's always quoting something or another. What's next?"

"Indeed, what was next?" Bess' voice took on a sultry note.

Sky lifted her head from Jaxon's chest. "Well first of all, you can quit sneaking around and tell me what's up."

"How did you know?"

She smiled down at Jaxon. "It's my business to know. Again, what's going on?"

The computer let out a sigh. "You are no fun. Maybe I should tell you just how gorgeous the one you call Zane's backside is. What do you think?"

Sky sat up, moving Zane out of the way as she reached for her clothes. "I think I'm going to lock you out of my bridge and definitely my quarters."

"You are just no fun suddenly, if you get my drift."

"Bess." Her voice carried a stern warning.

"The inverter has been fixed. I do think we will need to get the hyperdrive system thoroughly checked out when to our destination. It's been a while since I've had any repairs done and I think a checkup is in order."

"Fine. Anything else." She pulled her t-shirt over her head and stood, snapping her pants.

"I would say you need to brush up on your hand-to-hand combat skills. Something tells me you're going to need them."

She tugged her hair out from her shirt, wrapped it around her fingers and found a clip on the console. "What makes you think that?" Sky stood, gazing down at her beautiful men. She wished she had time for another round but the business at hand called. They would have more play time tonight once she taught them a few things about the ship, the place they were going and the world they would be entering.

"There's been a ship following us in another hyperspace envelope to the right of us. They are sufficiently back, which makes me believe they don't think we can see them. Good thing you upgraded the sensor array the last time in space dock."

"Damn." Her hands flew over the console to bring up the ships particulars. "I'm sure it's Jesata. Can we out run her? We need at least a half a galactic day before she gets to port."

"I don't know, boss. This is the first jump we've done in over a year and there's only been one on this new drive. I'm not sure how it will take the strain."

"Figure it out and get back to me. There are many items we need to contemplate before we go planet side."

"Have you figured out what port we're going to?"

"Haven't gotten that far, Bess. Why don't you run me all the reports and news you can find for the top three?"

"Righto, Captain."

"And give us a little more time. I'm sure there are questions." She arched her eyebrow toward the men who were now silently putting on their kilts and robes.

"Yeah, you could say we have questions." Jaxon adjusted his robe. "Please tell me you have something else we can wear."

A smile crossed her face as she watched them go back to their chairs. She pressed the button on hers to return to its normal form and sat down. "I have clothes."

"They aren't clothes for displaying our wares, are they?"

A slight snort left her mouth. "I have all sorts of men's wear. It just depends upon what you want. I have things which would make your outfits for the revue seem tame."

For the second time, Jaxon went pale. "Since we're with you, we won't need to be like your – your – slaves or anything? Right?"

"That's why I'm having Bess check out the latest on the three biggest space ports. I don't want to make you uncomfortable at all. It's enough you'll be totally out of your element in these places."

"Want to tell us what we'll be up against?" Zane crossed his arms and waited.

She observed them for a few moments, not sure how to answer them. This would be new and so very different from anything they'd ever done before. They needed to be prepared and she was the only one who could prepare them. "The ports I'm talking about each have close to a hundred-thousand full-time residents and five hundred times that many travelers passing through. I first want to study each of them to make sure there aren't any official meetings happening in any of them."

Jaxon nodded. "Good idea. It would be a logistics nightmare if we were caught in something like that. Will people be looking for you?"

The astute man had her intrigued and she recognized that he was more than he appeared. "If Bess is right and I'm really who Jesata wanted, we could be walking into more than any of us bargained for from the moment we arrive until we can leave the port."

"Can we have the documents already prepared and just file them?" Zane's expression was quite serious.

Sky nodded once. "Most of them. The packet isn't complete however until we fill out the last three in front of the official at the filing office."

"Will the filing set off any alarms to anyone?" Jaxon leaned forward.

"Not normally because Earth is considered a backwater rim world, at the very edge of the known universe. Notice I didn't say galaxy. People just don't come out here without a reason."

"And you wanted to lose yourself in the great unknown."

"In a way."

"What do you mean?"

"While it's true no one on my planet knew what was out here, we had identified certain areas where it was possible life supporting planets might exist. Earth has actually been visited by people from my planet thousands of years ago. Once it was realized the planet had nothing of value and no technological advancements, people were told to avoid it."

"I'm sure our world's governments will be happy to know we aren't important. That still doesn't explain why you ended up here." Jaxon's gaze bore into her while Zane watched her just as closely.

"I don't know. I guess I just felt this place was far enough off the beaten track I wouldn't be found."

"I get this place is far away from home and I get you didn't want to kill your mother. What I don't get is why you felt you couldn't overcome those obstacles."

She stared at Jaxon and Zane. These two would not let her off the hook easily and she had asked herself that very question. "Can I just answer I don't know for now? It's something we can explore once we have some free time later."

"But what if there isn't a later? What if Bess is right and this whole thing is designed to get you back to a place where your mother, or someone else, can eliminate or kidnap you?"

She wiped her hand over her face. Jaxon's mind went places she should have thought about. "I agree, we need to be prepared for the worst-case scenario." She sat back and leaned back her head. This was not going well at all. There were too many unknowns and these two counted in that group. She felt a pair of hands on her thighs and looked up as Jax's touched her.

"These are not insurmountable problems. We just need to get the logistics worked out to make sure we consider every contingency."

She dipped her head in agreement. "I agree but I just can't seem to get my mind settled on what I need to do." Sky gave him a wry smile. "You two have my normal sensibilities all fouled up."

"You're not too good for ours either," he admitted. "Is she, Zane?"

"No, she's not, but then again she doesn't know what we can or can't handle either."

She looked across the room and saw the unwavering glance of what was known on Earth as a warrior. She had been likened to one many times herself. "Who are you two?" Her confused gaze took in one then the other.

"Guess the gig is up, my friend," Jaxon threw back to Zane before turning back to Sky. "I think we should show you better than tell you. Do you have a room where you practice?"

"Practice what? I haven't had another humanoid on this ship for years and prey was never allowed to intermingle with myself."

"Again, och, you know how to put a man in his place." Zane frowned at her as he stood. "Just take us to what you have. I think you'll understand very quickly."

"I have a big room where I would hold general cargo. It should be big enough." She took one final glance at the console before getting up to lead the way. "Follow me."

Going to the stairs, she went down and turned left, past the airlock where prey was brought aboard and into a large empty room. "It hasn't been used for years. I hope this is what you had in mind." She made a sweep with her hand. "Bess did remind me I would need to get some paying galactic jobs if we had to stay out here. We might have to put this to use soon. Now just what is it you two have to show me?"

She turned and barely missed a fist to her jaw. "What are you two doing?"

"Showing you what our special skills are." Jaxon flexed and jumped about as if he were warming up his muscles. Zane did the same as he too danced around her.

Sky narrowed her eyes. She could play this game as well since she had been on the Tyrsatian sparring team, winning a championship her first year out. "Are you two sure you want to do this?"

Jaxon gave her a wicked smile. "Sure, why not?"

"Because I have enhancements."

"Explain enhancements, luvey." Zane took another swing at her and missed.

"Dim the lights for a moment, Bess." She looked at them and whirled her optics. "For one, this kind. I can watch prey and based upon his respiration, eye movements and a host of other things, figure out just which way he's going to jump."

"Impressive. Thanks, Bess."

The lights came back full strength. "Hey, when did you start taking orders from them?"

"They said thanks, Princess Xera."

Both men stopped in their tracks. "Did she just call you Princess?" Jaxon looked flabbergasted.

"I thought I heard her say Princess." A stern look crossed Zane's face.

Sky laughed her first true laugh in ages. Once they worked some things out, it appeared these two would be good for her. She immediately rushed in and did a one-two, knocking them both a little sideways. "First rule: don't let anything distract you."

They looked at each other and grinned. "She knows the rules, it would appear."

"Makes this so much more fun."

She wished she knew what they were talking about. Even without that advantage, she knew she was just as strong as they were. She moved with them, trying to keep one on either side of her. While her enhancements could help her in many ways, they were still taxed when faced with two opponents. She glanced from one and knew her mistake immediately as Jaxon rushed her. Flipping him over her back, she could not avoid Zane as he took her down. Wanting nothing more than to get herself out from under his tempting body, she shoved her hand in his solar plexus and sent him flying.

Sky barely had time to recover before Jaxon came toward her again. She scarcely managed to miss his fist as she realized his reach was at least six inches or more longer than her own. Somehow, she tossed a jab his way and connected with his body to send him to the ground. Zane was immediately there, throwing another punch and she took one in the side as he came on with gusto. She looked at his devastating grin and could feel her body respond. Her breathing became harder.

"This is fun," she stated and circled them both. "How long do you think we can keep this up?"

"Until one of us drops," Jaxon answered matter of factly.

A large grin filled her face. "Wow. I haven't done this since I was on the sparring team at home. Where did you get your training?"

"Special forces, luv." Zane continued to bounce around while Sky stopped in her tracks.

"Government trained?" she questioned before Jaxon's roundhouse kick hit her side. The hard kick took the air out of her lungs and she went down. Jumping up quickly, she glared at them both. These two were very serious. Grunting, she swung out with her left toward Zane, knowing she exposed herself once again to Jaxon. In a miracle move, she managed to punch and jump simultaneously, landing a kick to Jaxon's groin as he went down with a thud. "Crap? Are you alright?" She went down on her knee to make sure she didn't do any permanent damage.

Jaxon immediately stopped and grabbed her wrists. "Rule number two: don't be distracted by an enemy's apparent injury."

She struggled for a moment, her breathing ragged, and then found herself flat on her back with his lean hardness against her. "Where did you get these rules?"

"We made them up as called for by the situation."

She looked up at Zane, who now held her wrists flat to the floor. "What do you plan to do?" she whispered breathless.

"What do you want us to do?" Zane asked.

She gave them a wicked smile. "Everything."

.•••● ✳ ●•••.

Chapter 9

FIVE EARTH DAYS FROM when the journey had started, or rather more precisely the moment Sky transported Zane and Jaxon to her ship, she knew she was headed for trouble. Now, she didn't know what she would do without them as they had wormed their way into her heart and she hoped they had room for her as well. She couldn't even look at them without being turned on as she thoughtfully gazed at them sitting in the learning stations.

They were picking up the history and nuances of her world in the universe faster than she could have ever imagined. During this time, they'd had sex more than she ever realized possible as in the past she could take it or leave it. The more time they spent together, the more she realized their two species were very compatible.

Zane turned to her in a slow motion, his eyes bright. "You know what I want to do, don't you?"

She gave them a wide grin. "I do and while I agree with you, you both need to complete this session before we move on to more leisurely activities."

Since that first sexual encounter and the subsequent sparring, they'd spent every waking moment either preparing what might happen once they landed in their chosen destination or discovering each other's bodies. It scared her that they may not be ready for what was ahead. Sure, both men were highly trained and had only became dancers because it brought them to the United States. Combined with a huge paycheck, they had been doing very well for themselves in a country where they were considered a novelty.

Together, they had chosen Zephram on the planet Rumnata as the place in the Neadra Quadrant to file the required claim for the planet Earth. They'd studied the vids and all available news to come up with the place they thought they could slip in and out of most easily. Then came the arduous task of teaching Jaxon and Zane about the society they were entering. It would frown upon cocky, knowledgeable men and they were never to speak of their training or their relationship to Princess Xera. It was the type of information, which got one killed.

So lost in thought, she didn't realize Zane came to stand next to her. His slight touch at her temple drew her attention to his face. His slow lazy smile thrilled her as his fingers trailed down her face, touching the corner of her mouth then finished the journey by moving along her jaw to her earlobe. She shivered in anticipation at his unhurried movements. He ended by raising her chin then brushing his lips against hers in a light, tender brush.

"I'm finished with my lesson," he whispered seductively and pulled her from her seat.

Sky swallowed hard. They had always been together as a unit and she had a little trepidation of making love to just one. "Shouldn't we wait for Jaxon?"

He looked up from the screen and took off the headphone. "I'll be down in a minute or two. I have one small lesson to complete. You two go ahead. I'll catch up."

Sky nodded once and allowed Zane to pull her after him toward her quarters. In the hall, right before her door, he grasped her butt and turned her around. He pressed his hardness against her and she could feel every bulge on his luscious body. She knew almost every plane and angle of this man, wanting to know even more. His caresses became harder as one hand moved to rub her breasts through the thin cotton material while the other moved lower. Her pulse quickened as she thought of the pleasure to come. A moan escaped her and she knew for the first time just how much she wanted these men to control her.

He reached under her knees, picking her up to push her to the wall. She wrapped her legs around his waist and kissed him greedily, devouring all he gave. She could feel his hard cock just clothing away as he rolled his hips against her, her pussy weeping. This primal passion was more than pure lust and over the days, she had tried to come to grips with what it might be. She closed her eyes and remembered the sheer joy she felt at seeing them both beside her in the mornings when she woke. She loved the way they kissed her, the way they sucked her body and filled her multiplied her emotions and tantalized her senses.

Zane pulled away from her. "I want to be selfish and take you all on my own."

"I understand." She breathed heavily. "Maybe just some foreplay." While she taught them, they taught her the nuances of being human and making love. Every move was important in their eyes and she only hope she did the right thing as she wrapped her hands around him.

"I don't think he'll quibble with that." He unlatched the door and carried her inside, gently placing her on the bed. "Do you know just how sexy you are?"

She shook her head. Men weren't allowed to express their desire of the female form on her planet. But in private, she speculated life must be very different. Men had a need to dominate the situation and outside dominance was replaced with sexual dominance in the bedroom or brothel.

He tugged at her shirt. "Let's get this off. I want to kiss your boobs."

She didn't know until these two just how sensitive her breasts could be. Zane's mouth began to worship her orbs even before her t-shirt touched the bulkhead. She arched into him as his tongue brought her nipples into hard pebbles.

"I love the way you taste." He watched her as he rolled her aureoles between thumb and forefinger as he went from one breast to the other with tongue and mouth.

She slipped her hands under his shirt to tweak his own nipples and was rewarded with a gasp. "I like your chest too. Take off your shirt." She almost regretted the fact that she had clothes that fit them. The kilts they had had in their male revue would have been just perfect. Then again, she hadn't told them just how the replicator worked for making clothing. His shirt flew across the room and she licked her lips in eagerness. She couldn't wait to get her lips on his body.

Sky ran her hands up his chest, leaned in and gave a gentle suck on his small, flat nipples. She laved his body with her tongue as his sigh of satisfaction filtered through her senses. Taking her mouth with his, she caressed the inside of his mouth as her tongue warred with his. She flipped him over and pushed her hand down his pants, unbuttoning each rivet on the jeans in a slow seduction. She loved how they both looked in jeans, their asses more than a subtle temptation.

His hands tugged at her pants as well and soon they were in what she now knew was a classic position: the sixty-nine. His tongue licked her slick slit as her mouth caress this cock, the large mushroom head turning a dark purple. She'd never paid much attention to the parts of a man's anatomy but now knew a man's testes were as sensitive as her breasts. She took their heavy weight in her hand and gently squeezed, rewarded by his moan of pleasure.

"If you keep that up, lass, Jaxon won't make it here."

She grinned around his cock. "He'll make it." She took him into her mouth and rimmed the head of his penis. As she sucked, it grew even more as she used her hand to pump his shaft. It felt good in her mouth, not nasty like she'd been told as his feel and smell assaulted her senses in a good way. She got to him as evidenced by his grunts, groans and movements of his hips. He slowly pumped into her, slipping his fingers inside her as she released a slow keening moan. "That feels so good." Fissures of hot desire spread over her body, settling low in her belly, making her pussy drip even more. She was nearly ready to orgasm, trembling with the sheer effort to hold back what her body so desperately wanted to do.

Her soft cry sounded ragged to her ears as his tongue slid to her clit yet again. As if sensing she needed more, he thrust two fingers into her wetness, finger-fucking her with deliberate leisure, pulling them in and out. The pleasure began to build through her body and she knew it would be only moments before she orgasmed if he continued. As if sensing her closeness, he pulled his fingers out and his tongue slid down to her clit again as she cried out. Pleasure came in waves and nearly put her over the edge when she felt another hand on her. Sighing in satisfaction, she felt complete and opened her eyes to gaze at Jaxon leaning over her.

"You didn't think I forgot, did you?" he whispered and took her mouth in a rough kiss. "I want you to suck my dick."

He already had his clothes off and his member jutted rock hard from his body. She nodded and opened her mouth. His cock thrust gently inside and she immediately savored the tangy taste of his precum. Zane continued to lick her cunt but lifted a hand to gently stroke Jaxon's balls. She saw the exchange through slit eyes and knew there was something more they could do for her today. But now was her time and she wanted nothing more than to feel the sweet clench of her body as she reveled in the pleasure they gave her.

As if sensing what she needed, Zane's ministrations on her clit intensified, with his fingers returning to slid into her body. Her little breaths around Jaxon's cock were the only indication at the sensations lapping all over her body. It was as if his tongue and fingers knew her every need as they were rough when friction was needed to move her up a notch and soft when it became too much. His tongue and fingers slid in and out with gentle persuasion to fall over the precipice for her pleasure alone.

Jaxon's voice cut through the haze. "Do you know what I want?" His question came out in a ragged whisper.

She took in a little more of his cock, her tongue rimming him in tender strokes. "No...what do you want?"

"I want you to come. Then I can ram my big cock up your ass while you're still getting off." He looked down at her with intense eyes. "And if that doesn't do the trick, we'll do it again until you're just as turned on as I am."

"I guess the leaves me with the pleasure of her front hole." Zane's breath fanned out on her sensitive crotch. " Are you ready to fall over the edge, sweetheart?"

Sky nodded as she continued to work Jaxon's big cock with her hand and mouth. This was going to be intense and the stage was set for it to get even more so. Zane's hands and mouth pulled and plucked at her until she felt she could take no more. As if on cue, Zane slipped a finger up her ass and she fell over the edge. She felt the orgasm wash her away with feelings as the flames licked at her body. This was more intense than ever before and she moaned in pleasure.

They weren't done with her and Zane flipped her over on top of him, his cock entering her slowly, inch by inch. "It isn't over yet, sweetheart."

She helped him as best she could and lowered herself even further, murmuring incoherently as he seated himself even deeper within her. He felt huge and she was grateful for every inch as these two fulfilled her in a way she could never imagine until now. Zane waited there and she could feel Jaxon at her back.

"Are you ready for me, lass?"

The rich timbre of his voice gave her a slight shudder of pleasure. "Always."

His cock was larger than Zane's but filled her in unimaginable ways as the shear bliss of the moment registered in her mind as he slid forward in a measured stroke. This was what her body was made for, two men...two lovers...who made her feel like there was no one but her. They mattered and she would make sure nothing ever happened to them. Zane slowly circled his hips as Jaxon withdrew to push himself back in as joy enveloped her body. She hoped they felt as good as she did this moment. Gasping, her consciousness registered just how huge their cocks were as they both stretched and filled her.

Soon, Zane's cock scrapped against her inner hot spot, rolling his hips again to make himself go deeper. Jaxon thrust himself inside, wrapping his muscular body over hers as he too went in deep. Together they pushed every hot spot to near cosmic heights as she strained for completion. Each stroke of their hard cocks and touch of their bodies against hers pulled her tight, making her clit tingle even more. Each stroke was an art form she felt as a million fingers of feeling started to rush through her body, bringing her more pleasure than she ever imagined.

She let out a soft keening wail and pumped harder with them as their cocks filled her, one in, one out. Their grunts and groans of enjoyment spurred her on as she reached deeper within herself for her world to shatter in hopes of taking them with her. It came in a rush, like a thousand supernovas on the ebony blanket of the night. She screamed with the awareness of her body being pulled apart and thrust back together. Her movements became frenzied as she rode the cosmic wave of her orgasm. Within seconds, she heard their wails as they both thrust hard into her one final time.

Sky was spent and they fell together on her wide berth, breathing heavily. Running her fingers over their bodies, her sensitized core throbbed. Once would not be enough but this time she wanted to take a different tack. "Could I see you two kiss?" Their startled movements nearly dislodged her from the bed.

"Why would we do that?" Jaxon's voice sounded strange.

"Why not? I mean I saw you before I transported you and Zane lovingly ran his hand up your back then kissed the top of your head." She lay there frowning. "I did read that correctly, didn't I?"

Zane let out a big sigh. "If you know about us, then you know we're bisexual."

She chuckled into his chest. "Really? Is that what you're calling it now days?"

"Seriously, we like women as much as we like each other," Jaxon stated rather indignantly.

She turned to gaze at him thoughtfully. "I understand that but you two had a relationship before me. It was special and I don't want to be the one to spoil the feelings you had for each other."

"Who says you're spoiling it?"

Sky shrugged. "No one. I just know that we'll be in space for long periods of time. I know I get moody and won't always want sex. You two are strong, virile creatures who will need some sort of outlet every day. And I don't always expect you to use your hand in the shower or however the men of Earth masturbate."

······ ✳ ······

Chapter 10

A SILENCE HUNG IN THE air and Sky thought maybe she had said the wrong thing. "You have to understand. Space can be a place where one goes mad without another humanoid and sometimes with one. You must do whatever to take your mind off being in the middle of nowhere and not a planet in sight. There is nothing but your ship, your wits and yourself. If you're lucky a mate." She shifted to a sitting position. "I'm sorry if I made you uncomfortable. I just thought..."

"You thought correctly," Jaxon said roughly and moved his hand across her to caress Zane's chest. "We didn't want to make it difficult for you. We've known each other since we were schoolboys and care about each other a lot. We explored each other's bodies when there was no one else and discovered we like it."

"Being in the Special Forces put somewhat a damper on those feelings," Zane stated quietly. "It's why both of us left the service when we could. When the opportunity came to go to the States we decided to go."

A frown crossed her face. "I've never understood just what the hang up is about same sex relationships. It's encouraged a lot in a matriarchal society's because their society feels it's easier. A relationship is a relationship, sex is just the icing. And one really doesn't want to be alone on long space voyages like I said. I'm just thankful my hops have been relatively short. So, tell me a little more about your life." She hoped she wasn't prying but she needed to know everything, as she would be putting her life on the line for them just as much as she hoped they would do for her.

"You're really okay with this?" Jaxon asked her again. "In the few days we've been together I think we've both come to care for you. I don't want to do anything which will jeopardize our new relationship."

"I have to agree with Jaxon." Zane's hand pushed her hair behind her ear. "We never thought we'd find a woman who would be comfortable with us as we are."

She knew what they both were asking and while she was beginning to feel the same, she wasn't sure she was ready to put it into words. "I'm okay with this. I'm starting to have feelings for you as well. I think we might be a good mating group. We just need to see what's in store for us. I don't want to promise something I can't deliver. It might be the best thing for you to return to Earth."

Jaxon nodded. "I can respect that."

She watched them with a fascinated eye. This was something she'd never felt she would ever want to see. Then again, she'd thought she would never have a long-term lover let alone two at all. Too messy. Besides, there was her family to think about and she knew where her mother wanted her to be. On the throne after her death and most of the time that didn't include ready-made mating groups. Nevertheless, Sky didn't want to be Queen for any reason. She liked her life the way it was.

She'd fallen in love with Earth, otherwise, she wouldn't be here on this foolhardy mission. Though she wasn't ready to tell them what they wanted to hear, she knew she was falling love with them as well. She let out a big sigh and stopped to watch them yet again. The conversation must have been exactly the right thing to say to them as Jaxon rolled over her to get even closer to Zane.

"You don't mind, do you? If you do, we'll stop this right now and only be together in private. Some women get all weird with it." His violet eyes spoke volumes. It was obvious he didn't want to hurt her in any way.

"Of course, I don't mind. I wouldn't have suggested it otherwise." She sat up, moved toward the middle of the bed, and watched her two lovers kiss. She saw them press their long lengths into each other and knew it wouldn't be long before they were grabbing at each other like they all groped when together in this bed.

She watched Zane's hand reach out and stroke Jaxon down his back to cup his buttocks. "I've missed you," she heard him whisper. Just watching them was beginning to turn her on and she knew it wouldn't take long to get her fired up.

Zane leaned forward and kissed Jaxon's chest, his fingers swirling his flat nipples before he gave them a slight pinch. She wanted those fingers to be on her as well but she needed to give them some time together before she intruded on them.

Jaxon reached out and put his hands on Zane's shoulders, moving his hips in even closer. His cock stood fully erect and was mere inches from Zane's hand.

"You want this, big boy?" Zane questioned lightly and reached for his cock. The man's moan filled the cabin.

"That feels so good. The little touches here and there haven't been enough." His body squirmed in anticipation of Zane's touch.

"How about if I do this?" Zane questioned and positioned himself to take Jaxon's cock in his mouth. Before his tongue rimmed the huge purple head, he winked at Sky.

The sight of his mouth on Jaxon's dick made her so wet, she reached her hand down to touch her soaking pussy, scooting herself to lean against the bulkhead. The thrill of just watching them was more than she thought it would be, more than she hoped and she slowly worked around her clit with her fingers.

She could tell that Jaxon enjoyed the feel of Zane's tongue on him because he arched deeper into his mouth and moaned. Jaxon was trembling as he looked down at him pulling his huge cock in and out of full lips while his hips gyrating in circular motions.

"This is better than I remembered," he breathed harshly. "Take me deeper, man, much deeper."

Zane nodded and proceeded to pull him even more inside his hot mouth. This was so thrilling and different she never thought she'd be a part of something like this in her life. She swirled her fingers around herself and wondered if she should introduce the toys she had hidden in their bedside table. She realized quickly all she needed to do was watch them to get turned on, add in stroking herself and she found herself very excited.

Sky watched Zane's hand on Jaxon's cock as he firmly pulled up and down on the hard shaft while stroking his thumb over the purple mushroom head. His cock grew even more under the gentle ministrations of his male lover. The scent of sex filled the small space and nearly overwhelmed her senses as she breathed in the rich sent. She watched as Zane moved his hand up to cup his tightened balls, heard another moan of pleasure. Continuing its upward journey, his hand swept across Jaxon's chest and encountered the hard nub of a nipple. His thumb and forefinger closed around the bit and pinched slightly, much like she had done over the past few days.

Jaxon's moan became louder. "Which way do you want to do this?" His accent was thick and made her tingle even more.

"Either way man." Zane murmured, his mouth still stroking cock.

He gave Sky the critical eye for a moment. "I want you in me while I'm in her. That's what I want. We've never tried it that way before but I'm sure we'll both get the satisfaction we need."

"As long as I get to do the same later."

"Let's ask her."

Two sets of eyes, one violet, one blue, turned to her in mid-stroke and she imagined the picture made with her leg over the arm of the chair, fingers in her cunt, hoping she made an enticing picture. "Sounds good to me," she answered in a breathless whisper. "Just tell me what you want me to do."

"Why don't you watch Zane get my dick a little harder then slide his up my ass? I'll let you know when to get under me. I just want to feel him inside me before I feel me in you." He stared at her a moment more. "And keep working yourself. It turns me on."

She nodded once, twirling her fingers yet again around her hard nub. "Do you want me to get off?"

"No," he grunted thrusting his hips yet toward Zane's mouth, his shaft going in a little deeper. "That's all for me, baby."

She smiled and spread her vulva for them to get a better view. "All yours then," came her hoarse comment.

"I wish you two would shut up."

Zane crawled up Jaxon's body, kissing the pliant flesh the whole way, stopping to churn his tongue around his nipples. Jaxon gave a whimper of approval as he pulled his head closer to him. Zane gave his chest another kiss, moved up to his neck and settled on his mouth. She could see his wet tongue surging inside as his hand was under Jaxon's jaw to hold him in place. She now saw the skill these two had in lovemaking and it was no wonder she was held captive to their charms. The experiences they'd provided her thus far were like no other.

Zane continued to kiss Jaxon for a few more minutes while stroking the man's cock until the head glistened with precum. "You know the drill," he barked sharply. "I want to be in you now."

Without another word, Jaxon flipped over and presented his ass to Zane. His eyes darkened, as he looked at her while Zane's fingers started to caress his backside. "I just love your ass but we definitely need some lube." He turned blue eyes toward Sky. "Where do you keep it?"

"See the button on the wall to your left? Push it and a bedside drawer will come out. You should find what you need in there." She stroked her wet body yet again, feeling the tingle of anticipation as she waited to join them.

Zane pressed where she had indicated and looked up at her in surprise. "These were there the whole time?"

Not trusting her voice, she nodded. "We'll be making good use of them now I know you have them."

"What?" Jaxon groaned.

"She's been holding out on us, Jax. She has a whole drawer full of toys."

"Good for her. I just want to feel your dick in my ass and my dick in her. Hurry up."

"As you command."

She watched as Zane squeezed out an ample amount of lubrication down Jaxon's crack. Tossing the tube back in the drawer, he smoothed his hand down the slick surface and rimmed his anus. The man practically went nuts. Patiently, Zane took some of the lube and stroked his dick with it.

"Just a second, man. You don't want me going in there dry." Another stroke and Zane was poised behind Jaxon. Again, he looked at her and smiled. "You're hot and I love looking at your cunt." He slid into Jaxon's body as he pushed back toward him. "God, I forgot how tight you are."

Jaxon grunted and let him seat himself completely, balls against ass. "Me too." He shuddered, as it seemed Zane's cock put some type of internal pressure on him sending him to nirvana as it made his cock leak even more. She frowned slightly wondering what happened.

Seeing her confusion, he smiled. "Men have a hot spot as well called the prostrate. You can't get to it any other way except through your ass."

"That's not quite true," Zane groaned as he slid in and out of Jaxon's ass. "The other way, you just don't get any pleasure from it."

"Oh." She continued to stroke her body as they slowly started to move, Zane pulling back, surging back in to the rhythm of Jaxon's heavy breathing. Every time his inner spot was hit, it was like a jolt of electricity went through him. His head went back as his grunts became louder. Just watching made her own body a tangled web of need. Her fingers started to move faster.

"No you don't," Jaxon groaned. "Get over here right now."

Her eyes got wide and she moved quickly. "Where do you want me?" His violet eyes, dark with ecstasy compelled her to give him what he wanted quickly. He licked his lips and gave her a wicked grin.

"Where do you want it, lass?"

Her breath hitched. "Where do you want it?"

"Where do you think?" She positioned herself in front of him and wasn't surprised when he leaned in to lick her tight rosette with unhurried preciseness. His tongue rasped across the sensitive flesh a few times as her hips went in drawn out rotations. "I'm just moving the lube around, girl." He grabbed her hips to keep her still and pulled her closer to fondle her breasts before sliding his long fingers to her slick folds.

She moaned in pleasure and rotated her hips again in a leisurely manner as his fingers moved in both of her holes, pulling moisture from one to the other. Leaning down on her elbows, her ass high, she just wanted him to stick his cock into her, to feel him glide in and out of her body, not caring where. "Please – please – I want your cock in me." Her voice came out in a breathless whisper, all tight and needy.

"I'm getting there," Jaxon ground out through clenched teeth.

She couldn't see them anymore but she could hear the sounds as flesh pounded flesh, all wet and wild. "If you don't fuck me soon, you'll miss your opportunity. And I know you love to be in me when I get off."

"Fine. Zane, let up a little." His thumbs spread her butt cheeks and pushed inside her tight rosette to make sure she was ready. He pulled her back to him and lined up, pushing his pulsating cock into her rear in a deliberate, firm stroke. She gasped as he stretched her, moving inside the tight ring of flesh. Once fully inside, he stayed in place. "Your butt feels like a glove, meant for big dick."

Her breath came in heavy gasps. "It feels – wonderful – and it's not going to take much."

Jaxon pressed his body over hers, his hand going to her clit, skimming the sensitive flesh with his long fingers. "How does this feel?"

"Like I'm standing on the edge of the cliff."

"Are you two ready?" Zane's voice purred and he surged forward.

Jaxon's hoarse cry was the only thing, which preceded the onslaught as flesh slapped against flesh. Harsh moans filtered through her mind as she realized the only thing she could concentrate on was her ass and his finger against her cunt. Reaching up, she stroked her breast as it tightened in expectation. Jaxon's hand felt her other one and pinched the nipple.

"Are you ready, girl?"

"I'm not quite there yet," she breathed.

"The hell you aren't," he whispered against her ear as his tongue rimmed it.

His hard cock heaved into her again as he squeezed her clit between his thumb and forefinger. She almost screamed and was seeing stars when Zane's hands joined his to tweak and pull her. Soon, she was a quivering mass of desire as Jaxon thrust into her deeper than before as a cry was torn from her lungs. She was flung to the far reaches of the universe and for once, she didn't care if they were with her or not.

She felt weak and wanted to curl up as the feelings were so intense but Jaxon was still in her, pushing in and out. She could feel his balls tighten where they hit her on her ass over and over, as he made one final shove to force himself even deeper within her. Without warning, she was soaring again, screaming her pleasure this time, holding onto the sheets tight. Jaxon's wail followed her quickly and she felt his cum deep within her.

Zane was still moving but quickened his pace upon hearing them. Driving his huge shaft in and out of Jaxon, allowed Sky to feel every move and she still tingled. She never thought it possible to have more than one orgasm yet these two provided the impossible daily. He savagely grabbed her breast as she glimpsed him biting down on Jaxon's shoulder before he cried his release.

They all collapsed in a maze of arms and legs, her sandwiched in the middle when Zane eventually moved to her front. She wanted to remember every nuance of this moment to file away should they depart ways in the future. She closed her eyes, knowing she needed to give them the choice even though she knew she could force them to stay with her in her world.

They had to choose her, otherwise, she needed to take them back to Earth because she couldn't bear to be with them in a sexless relationship. This turned her world upside down and she never needed anything more than she needed these two men.

It scared her to death to think she needed something more than just herself to survive.

Chapter 11

"ARE YOU ALL SURE you have the plan down?" Bess had asked this question at least a thousand times and it wore thin.

"We're as ready as we can be. We have all the documents except for those I have to sign in front of the magistrate."

Sky glanced back at Jaxon and Zane all decked out in their kilts standing patiently behind her. They had the classic version, which draped over their bare chests and down their backs. She was surprised when they had chosen these outfit yet the other choices were even more auspicious when she thought about it. They had both decided to go with their clan kilts and it took a few tries before the clothing replicator got it right. Still, it grated on her that they would be looked upon as her possessions and needed to be on display for the other women of the port. She closed her eyes and took a deep breath. Just let one of those biddies try to touch either one.

"Are you all right?" Zane had stepped closer to her.

"I'm fine. I just don't know what we'll be going into exactly and it bothers me. Bess, has that other ship requested port permission?"

"They just did." Her voice had a soothing quality today. Over the time they were all together, she had taken a shine to her boys, teaching them everything she could.

"Was it Jesata as we suspected?"

"It is but it's not her normal ship."

"We need to have the specs on that ship before we leave port. If we can't blow her out of the sky, I need to know."

"Yes, Captain. Anything else before we dock?"

She chewed on the inside of her lip. "You've check the corridor immediately outside the lock, right?"

"Like I said, no one is there. Besides, you three have enough concealed weapons to take out a small army."

"And they won't try to take them away?"

Bess gave a snort of laughter. "Hardly. These people are pirates from all places including some male dominant planets. We've used your old registration as a Harvester ship to gain access. The codes are still good as you originally registered them for your lifetime plus fifty years. The most I expect to happen to you is that you might be questioned heavily about your mother. The news from Tyrsati has all been good and nothing is out of the ordinary."

"You're sure their universal translators have all the languages we can possibly encounter here. We can't have them saying the wrong thing." She gave them a wry smile.

"We've practiced and I've checked it a thousand times, awake and asleep. I've even checked your drazee because I knew you wouldn't."

She'd forgotten the little creature attached to her wrist. It was such a part of her it was hard to forget it was actually a living being that did her will by providing her with a weapon and all the technology she wanted in a handheld. "Thanks."

"You're welcome. I wish you'd quit being so nervous. There is nothing here, which could hold you at all. Especially once they find out who your mother is."

"Any other news you need to impart?" She stalled as she didn't want any of them to be in danger but knew she had no other choice. She also didn't want to risk the chance of her mother getting involved.

"Sky," Jaxon rubbed her shoulder gently. "We're ready for this. We need to get it done and over."

She nodded once. "Lockdown security code 5-niner-two-six. Only the boys or I can release you. Remember the word?"

"Oh, yeah," came her sexy reply.

Sky turned and walked toward the lock. She took one more appreciative glance at them before she moved on. This had to be by the book or someone might just notice and realize just how valuable her prey was. Keying a code on the pad, she waited for the air to cycle before the door swung open. She almost gagged as she forgot just what a space dock smelled like. This one was absolutely ancient with new sections added as needed so the air circulation tended to be poorer in the oldest areas.

There was absolutely no paint on the stark grey bulkheads and the rivets appeared slightly rusty. The seals were obviously holding, as she didn't hear the hiss associated with escaping air. That would be a reason to ask for another berth if she ever heard the vacuum of space sucking out the breathable atmosphere.

She glanced both ways down the corridor, noting much the same either way and took a right, her dark coat flaring as she turned. Flanked on either side by what appeared to be bodyguards, she knew they made a formidable team. She moved with more confidence than she would have expected when first coming back to her unpredictable part of space. Her head held high, they didn't see another soul until they reached the cross point where they were formally admitted to the station. Security seemed high, as there were two guards, one with a gun, and another to look over their papers. He held out his hand the moment she was close enough.

"Nature of your business in Zephram?" His voice held a slight nasal sound and she knew he was from one of the male dominant planets. They all had the same nasal accent.

"To file a Harvester claim." Her self-assured voice carried throughout the tunnel, echoing softly.

"This is a little far out to be submitting that type of paperwork, don't you think?"

Sky nodded once. "I agree. I'm claiming a planet on one of the outer rims and a challenge was issued. You were the closest place."

"I didn't realize you Harvesters still issued challenges to each other what with the breaking up to the central core and all."

She kept her surprise to herself. "I've been on the outer rim for a long time. I didn't realize there were any changes to the laws."

"There aren't really. They're licensing more than just the females as Harvesters any more. That just happened last year after the Menos Prime incident."

She narrowed her eyes, her drazee pulsating on her wrist and felt the men press closer to her back. "I'd heard that was a plague."

He nodded. "It was but they discovered it was genetically engineered, which put them in a bad position. They decided to license both sexes as Harvesters. From what I understand, it was a chaotic situation for months until they could get what few men they had back under control. They gave them each the same opportunity but only a few made it through the grueling Harvester trials."

She tried to keep her breathing steady. Parts were settling into place as to the mystery of why Jesata was in the outer rims. Sky looked up and smiled as he handed her papers back to her. "Thanks. Are the offices still located in the M2XC off the main corridor? It's been quite a while since I've been here."

"Yes. Just keep going straight, make the first left and follow the signs. They should have you out of there in no time."

She turned back to look at them. "Come on, we don't have time to waste," she stated rather gruffly. She needed to get them to a private area where they could talk. She moved fast and expected them to follow. She found the filing office in no time but went past it to what appear to be a bar. Sky moved to the doors and looked in from side to side. Satisfied, she swung open the door and went to the counter.

"I need a privacy room, high security please." Her fingers tapped the counter impatiently.

The woman took in her and glanced at the men behind her. "In for a little play time, Harvester?"

"Not today. We just need a quiet place where we can get a drink and discuss life."

Confusion crossed her face. Sky knew most Harvesters would sample their wares in a place like this for the public to see. It would help with the sale of their stock. She glared at the woman who was just doing her job. "Don't ask. I'm in a private type of mood."

"Sorry, lady, didn't know you were a VIP."

"I don't try to throw my weight around. I just need a few moments before we go to the magistrate."

Her eyes gleamed. "I get it now. I take it you won't need it more than an hour?"

Sky shook her head. "An hour would be more than enough." When the clerk held up the pad for her Ident card, she ran her wrist with the drazee over it. Her heart jumped as it took moment but the system registered them without giving up who they were. Thank god for Bess.

"First door on the right. I've given you one with a front window so you can see when the magistrate arrives. There's always the chance you'll want to put on a show for us. We have so few of them now."

Shock filtered through her system. She had just assumed the person would be available when they arrived. "They aren't in? The magistrate that is."

The clerk chuckled. "They go out every morning for their chai at this time."

"Thanks." Sky went to the booth indicated and walked in followed closely by the men. Once they were all inside, she cycled the system and waited for the green light to indicate the security was on before turning to lean on the door. "We're in trouble."

Both Jaxon and Zane stood in the center of the room frowning, watching her intently. Zane was the first to move to the couch on the far wall. "Then we need to appear to be having a quiet interlude. Why don't you two come and sit next to me?" He patted the couch next to him.

She sighed, shrugging her shoulders at Jaxon before moving to sit next to him. "What the hell...it can't get any worse."

"Are you trying to curse us, lass?" Jaxon asked as he settled next to her, thigh touching hers.

"No, of course not."

"Then just what is the problem?" Zane's fingers moved her hair behind her ear and turned her face toward him as his fingers continued their gentle strokes down her face to her neck.

"Bess was right. This was never about you. It was all about me." She shook her head wondering why she was so stupid.

"Explain it to us," Jaxon wrapped his arm around her shoulder, making her feel snug and secure.

"You heard what the guard said at the portal check. Menos Prime decided to license both men and women as Harvesters. Bess had told me that they were moving more toward a planet with equal rights. If that happened, my mother and her cronies would have declared war on them to make sure it doesn't happen."

Jaxon looked at her stunned. "Why would she do that?"

Sky shook her head in disbelief. "Matriarchal society doesn't mean no balls. If I've learned anything over the years, it's been about my mother's fearless nature. She acts first then thinks about it later. She wouldn't hesitate to bring a lesser ruler back in line. She truly thinks if men were in power, they would ruin the world and in some cases, I'm sure she's right. Though it really doesn't matter when it comes right down to it, people are horrible to others no matter what their sex. Harvesting taught me that."

Zane gazed at her thoughtfully. "I didn't realize your mother was that powerful."

"There's only one queen more powerful than her and luckily for both of them, they've been friends for years."

"This still doesn't explain to me why we're in trouble." Jaxon scowled at her.

She leaned forward putting her chin in her hands. How could she have been so naive? "When this all started, I just thought it was Jesata challenging me because I had bested her so many times over the years."

"And now?"

Their gentle rubs warmed her back. "Imagine the impact I would have as a political prisoner."

Their hands stopped. "There's something you've not told us, isn't there?" Zane leaned down to look at her face.

"Yeah, there's something I haven't told you." She scratched her head. This was definitely not good.

"Should you have told us before we came inside the station?" Jaxon's voice held a deadly quality.

She turned to him and saw his hard glare. "Probably but given what I thought, what we all thought, about the situation, I didn't think it was important at the time."

"Exactly what are we talking about here? Did you vaporize a planet or something? Are you wanted for some horrible crime?" Zane's eyes questioned her silently.

She gave a soft chuckle. "No, nothing like that. I'm not wanted for murder or anything bad. Matter of fact, there would be only one person who would want me back."

"Then what is it?"

She let out a long sigh. "I'm the heir apparent to my mother's wealth and kingdom and lifestyle."

They blinked. "And you think Jesata wants to capture you to ransom you to your mother?"

She nodded. "It would be the perfect ploy and something that would get my mother's attention."

"Why would Jesata even consider doing this?"

"Because she worked for Queen Akira of Menos Prime. The woman funded every one of her expeditions."

Zane sat back. "Well that puts a new twist on things."

"And makes our position even more tenuous. I can bet Jesata fabricated this whole thing just to get you here."

"I just don't understand how she found me in the first place."

Jaxon nodded. "Maybe it was just a lucky guess. Didn't you say that you had contacted your family when you upgraded Bess?"

She shook her head. "No, it had been five years since I actually let my mother know I was doing well. The whole situation is just too complicated and I was tired of being a pawn in a system I didn't want to rule."

"I see where you're going with this, Jaxon." He turned back to Sky. "From where did you place this last communication?"

"A place called Geioto Omego. It's totally in the other direction from here, there was no way she could have placed me in the outer rim like she did."

"Now think about it, Sky. You said yourself you always like short jumps. Was this information Jesata knew as well?"

She leaned back into the couch and rubbed her eyes. Crap, she didn't even want to think about it. "During one of my first Harvest runs, Jesata and I ran into each other in a bar in the Destry galaxy. She was bragging about how long she could stay in space. I had told her I didn't like being alone that long at all."

"I think you have your answer. All she would have had to do is to calculate short jumps from your last communication to possible habitable worlds."

She stared at Jaxon. "How could I have done that?"

"It was a bar, Sky. People say things when they've had a few drinks in them."

"And I was young. It was probably my first or second Harvest run." Her head hurt. They would have to fight to get out of here even if she did file her claim. "I hate that woman. It made me wonder if being alone wasn't what made her cruel."

"No, those people are like that from birth. Makes me sad that she had all those men to torture."

"I agree, Zane. BDSM can be a sexual turn on but when used to bring pain and mental trauma no one wins. Those men were probably damaged beyond repair."

"Or they exacted their own special torture." She sighed deeply. This was a little more complicated than she expected. "The other thing that has me a little worried is the fact that Queen Akira allowed men obtain Harvester licenses."

Zane puffed up. "Why? Don't think we could do it?"

"No, that's not it at all. I fear she's found some male strong arm who is just as cruel as she is. Now not only will broken men be put on the auction block but women as well. No one deserves that type of life. No one."

.... ✳ ...

Chapter 12

THEY SAT THERE IN silence for a few moments when Sky saw an entourage enter the office next door. "It looks like the magistrate is back. Let's get this done." She gave each of them a heartfelt look, got up and walked to the door to enter their code once again, relieved when the door snickered open. She moved out to the lobby, nodding toward the clerk and went into the corridor with the men close behind.

Sky hesitated in front of the magistrate's door. This would change everything and she was a fool to think it wouldn't. By doing this act of protection, the Earth would be hers to watch, although silently. She didn't want to upset the delicate balance of the life there. They had enough problems of their own without her adding to them. Then there was her relationship with Zane and Jaxon. That too was a delicate balancing act and she only hoped they understood why she was doing this in the first place.

Opening the door, she strode in, happy to see they were the first ones there. She proceeded to the counter and waited impatiently. Finally, a clerk came over to them, inquiring about their need.

"I have the papers to file a Harvester claim. I need to get this done today."

The man's eyebrows arched in surprise. "Wow, that will be three this week. What world would this one be for?"

She stood there stunned. "This one would be for Earth. Who else have been making claims?"

The clerk glanced back to the main office and leaned over the counter to whisper. "I'm not supposed to be saying anything but there was a princess from the Tyrsatian worlds in earlier in the week, then waiting for us this morning was someone from the Menos Prime area. We're having a regular run-on claims this week!"

She kept her face as emotionless as possible. One of the sisters had finally made it to Harvester level and this shocked her more than anything. When she had left, all of them had been in the frilly girl stage and not a one wanted to go into the family business. "I see." She glanced back at the men who merely shrugged. "No one has made a claim on Earth."

The man straightened, his voice still hushed tones. "No claim has been made on any rim worlds that I know of at all. The claim this morning was somewhere in the Destry galaxies and the one early in the week was in the Katan galaxy where the plague was. I found it rather odd at the time."

She took in a slow breath. Not if you're making a political statement...what an easy way to take over. She would need to discuss this with the guys later as the implications were enormous.

"I see. Can we just process this one quickly, if you don't mind? We need to get supplies and get back to our claim. You know what happens when a lot of Harvesters are in the same vicinity."

He chuckled and stood completely. "So I've heard. You have all the standard documentation...correct?"

She nodded. "I have everything my computer could find. I've been out of touch for a while and don't know if there are any new document requirements."

The man gave her an odd look then. "You do have all your credentials still intact...right?"

Sky gave him a brilliant smile. "Of course, I do. Just because I haven't been around doesn't mean I'd give up something so important. It took me years to get those and they cost many galactic credits. I'd be a fool to not keep those current."

A slight shake of the head showed his agreement. "A small kingdom's worth from what I hear." He took the papers and headed back to the magistrate's office. "Let me show him and we'll get your final paperwork completed in a jiff."

She turned back to Jaxon and Zane. "Did you two get any of the conversation we whispered?"

Zane shook his head. "Just bits and pieces...what's going on?"

She ran a nervous hand through her hair. "It seems they've had a run on claims this week. One was probably Jesata just this morning and the other..."

Jaxon gave her a concerned look. "Who was it, Sky?"

"My sister. I didn't get which one but it makes me wonder why she was out here so far from home. Her claim was in the Destry galaxy."

"What does this mean for us?" Zane questioned quietly, his eyes on the door behind her.

"I don't know." Her worried look didn't escape them and both took her hand to rub her gently.

"It will be okay. Nobody has said anything out of the ordinary to us so far."

Jaxon's eyes held hers fast. She shook herself mentally. He was right, they had nothing to worry about. She heard footsteps behind her and turned to see a rotund man waddle toward her. "Everything in order?"

He set her application on the counter before turning his beady eyes upward. "This Harvester code is very old."

"I haven't used it in eight years. If you note, it has been renewed yearly per the requirements. I've just moved around so much and finally found a planet I want for my own. Is anything else out of order?" She could hear her heart pounding in her chest.

"You have the required fee?"

Thank god, the man was all business only she knew it would be taking a chunk out of her galactic credits. She didn't want to transfer any from the account her mother had setup for her as it would alert her to where she was. "Of course. Has the fee gone up while I was gone?"

"Just the standard five percent. Do you plan to make this new claim your primary residence?"

This was new. "Possibly. Their society is already set in place and I had decided discreteness was best. No need to have a planet wide panic set in."

"Isn't that the truth?" The man flipped through the papers once again, pulled out the last page. "Your signature is required before the application is complete. As required, you are to sign in my presence." Sky bobbed her head and picked up the pen. She wrote her standard galactic name with flourish then turned the paper back toward the man. He glanced down at the signature becoming immediately flustered. "Princess, excuse me, I didn't know." He began to bow when she grabbed his wrist.

"Don't please. I left that life long ago by my own choice. It's just Sky now. No one is to know I've been here...is that clear?"

He eyed her cautiously. "Whatever you desire, Princess. This will be filed immediately once you pay the fee. Do you have a chip I can put your copies on?"

She lifted her wrist with the drazee and heard the computers engage then beep when the transaction was complete along with her copies safely secure in the device. With a smile, she turned toward the men before throwing the magistrate a fleeting look. "Can you tell me which one of my sisters was here?"

"I just finalized the application yesterday. I believe it was Princess Myka."

She rotated back toward the door. "Thank you, magistrate. I've enjoyed doing business with you." Indicating to the men, it was time to go, she hurried into the corridor. Now all they needed was some luck to get back to the ship quickly. Supplies would have to wait for another trip. They wouldn't starve before they got back to Earth but the rations wouldn't be as top notch as normal. "We need to get out of here quickly."

"Is there another way out of here? We'd be less suspicious that way." Zane asked as he walked close behind her.

She shook her head. "I don't know. Let's ask, Bess." Lifting her hand up, she punched in the codes. "Bess, I need to know if there is another way out from our currently location."

"Let me check for you. Are you in trouble?"

"Not yet but something tells me we'll be in a world of hurt here in a few minutes." She impatiently tapped her foot and scanned her surroundings. The station was waking up and more people were milling around the upper corridors. She leaned over the rail and looked at the promenade, lots of people getting supplies or any number of things as all the shops were open. Glancing at the guys, she was happy that they too were keeping a sharp eye on their surroundings.

"Sky, the only way to the ship is the way you came. I can't even find a series of ducts for you to crawl to me. There was just no extra space in these older stations for the escape routes and the like."

Strike down any sneaking out of the place. "What's the corridor look like?"

"That's where it's odd. I've patched into the station's cams and the guards you went by are still in place but they've let a few other people in while you've been gone. Some went to other ships but the others, I think someone's planning an ambush but I can't get a good tag on who it might be."

"Jesata." Sky let out an angry harsh breath. "Anything you can do to help us."

"Nada. The station's systems are locked down tight. There isn't even a back door as far as I can see. Sorry, kid, but this time it seems you're on your own."

She pounded her fist against the rail. This was exactly what she hoped to avoid. "We're on our own and the way back is the way we came in. Bess says the corridor is hiding an ambush. Any thoughts?"

Jaxon nodded. "It's not unexpected, Sky, with everything you've told us. One of us should go in first..."

She cut him off. "I should go in first just in case it isn't me they want. I have the drazee and it can raise a deflection shield if I need it. You have no such weapon in your arsenal. I think your best action would be stealth."

"Fine, we'll play it your way. Do you always get so grumpy before a fight?" Jaxon asked.

She let out a huff. "I hate fighting. I've always hated it even when it was just me and my sisters. It's why I left home. I didn't want to kill one of them or my mother for the throne. It just creeps me out that some of the houses still are feudal that way."

Zane stared at her. "It's good you're getting all this old baggage off your chest. For your information, no soldier worth their weight likes war or fighting. Sure, some men get off on it because we're programmed that way but it doesn't mean the majority of us like it. Get your game face on and let's go."

Her eyes got wide as she gawked at him. No one had ever dared to tell her to get it together. "Did you just command me?"

Zane gave her a brilliant smile. "I knew that would get you going. You're useless to us unless you're focused. Ready?"

She gave him another glare before a quick nod. "You're right. Make sure all your weapons are armed and ready. We'll be there in less than five minutes."

Unlike before, the place teamed with life as people moved in and out of their way. She kept her eyes moving and felt the men's presence at her back, knowing they did the same. It seemed as if people were staring at her although she knew it was more the way they looked. One female Harvester in all black and men in kilts, which had never been seen in this quadrant she was sure, had to make a larger than life picture. People scattered to get out of their way if they caught the look on their faces.

In only minutes, they were at the guard station. The guards didn't even ask for credentials but just waved them through. Odd, it used to be papers were checked coming and going. Maybe the magistrate alerted them to her status. Sky stopped anyway. "My ship's computer alerted me a lot of activity on this corridor."

Both guards looked at her in surprise. "We've only allowed those who came from this portion of the station back inside. Did your ship tell you anything was amiss?"

She gave them a wry smile. "She didn't know what was up...just that it made her uncomfortable. If you hear any shooting please notify the magistrate. I'm sure he'll be interested." That would at least give them backup if they needed it, not ideal, but some.

"Would you like us to accompany you?" the one with the gun asked.

She shook her head. "No, we'll be fine. We're armed in the usual manner. I just was hoping to avoid anything."

"I understand. We'll keep our eyes and ears open."

"Thanks." A brusque jerk of her head and she walked through the door, allowing all her senses to open. There were things about her the boys still did not know, as a girl always needed secrets. They knew she had some enhancements but this one was natural. Standing still, she allowed data to pour into her from every empty space and cubbie within the long corridor. Her eyes focused on two hatch halls three doors before theirs or about roughly two hundred feet from their current position.

The men stood quietly behind her as her intent gaze went around the space in front of them. Only when one of them shifted restlessly, did she come out of her near trance. "There's someone hiding in the two hatch halls halfway down."

"Did your eyes tell you that?" Jaxon asked quietly.

She turned to them, her optics whirling. "No, my senses did."

"You'll have to explain later. Plan?" Zane questioned.

"I'll walk down the center, you hide in the hatch halls and come up behind me but slowly, keeping to the edges if possible. I'll be going very deliberate, so there will be no rush to keep up with me. Make sure each of those halls are empty before moving to the next. I want to make sure whoever they are, they can't surround us." She didn't wait to hear their reply, just started up the hall with a steady pace when the hairs rose on the back of her neck.

Someone stepped out into the center of the corridor. "Well, look who made it in time."

"Jesata. Nice to see you here." She tried to siphon through the data coming at her to discern how many were with her but something blocked her.

"Can't quite pick us up, can you?" An evil smile crossed the woman's face as she fingered the laser at her hip. "I know all the secrets too. Courtesy of you if I remember."

Damn her youth yet nothing in her made her move from her precarious position. "What do you want?"

"What makes you think I want something?"

Sky smile and took a casual stance. "You always want something, Jesata. I've never known you to act otherwise."

"Everything." Her gun came up in a flash and she fired a single shot.

••• ✳ •••

Chapter 13

S KY MOVED SLIGHTLY TO the right then glanced quickly at her long leather coat to see a hole. "You put a hole in my best leather, Jesata. Whatever were you thinking?" She frowned at the woman in front of her who stood stunned. "It looks like you thought you hit me. Fie on you."

"There's plenty where that came from," Jesata sneered.

Sky moved her head side to side. "I don't think so. If you want me and my men, you'll have to fight me for it." A wicked gleam came into her eyes. "Are you sure you really want to do that?"

"We have enough people to take you," she muttered.

A groaned could be heard behind her. "Really? Sure about that?" Sky took a step forward.

Jesata waved her gun wildly. "Stay back. I know what you are."

"No one knows what I am. I think I even scared my mother." Her calm voice seemed to soothe the woman's frantic movements. "Now don't you just want to leave me alone?"

"Stop trying to play your mind tricks on me, woman, just fight me straight up then." Jesata took a step forward.

"Fine, call off your dogs before my men finish them. We don't need any stray laser fire in this older corridor. It could have catastrophic results." She impatiently tapped her foot. Sky knew it was imperative to keep control, as the outcome would be bad. She quickly closed her eyes to make her optics stop whirling then opened them to see Jesata just a few feet away, her gun pointed directly at her chest.

Moving faster than the eye could see, she took the gun and redirected it back toward the infuriating woman. "I told you not to point that damn thing anywhere in this corridor...didn't I make myself clear?"

The woman gawked at her ineptly. "How – how did you do that?"

She cocked her head to one side. "Family secret. Try to hit me. Please, I want this over with as quickly as possible." The red-faced anger of Jesata was almost comical as her hand moved to strike her. Sky sidestepped it adeptly. "Is that all you got?" She understood she really shouldn't make the woman blow a gasket but she needed to teach her a lesson she would long remember and convey to other Harvesters.

"I've got enough to take you, bitch." She took another swing but Sky easily moved out of her way.

"Are you sure about that?" Sky threw her hands out in submission. "I don't want you to hurt yourself here."

"Arghhh," screamed Jesata as she rushed her.

Sky decided to stand her ground this time and let Jesata push her a little up the corridor. A quick karate chop to the woman's shoulder and she dropped one arm as she struggled to get another punch in. "Done yet?"

"Sky Xera Nerezsh, quit playing with that woman and finish the job." A voice from one of the corridors commanded.

She knew that voice and was filled with dread. "Sorry," she whispered softly to Jesata and pressed her hand against her solar plexus, flinging her down the corridor toward the voice. Although the woman appeared to be hit hard, she bounced softly on the wall and slid down the bulkhead. Sky stood her ground. "Mother, I didn't know you were on this space station."

The woman came out of a hall just past where Bess was docked. "You don't know a lot of things, Daughter. Have your sister bring you to the cruiser within the hour." She turned without another glance, her cream-colored coat flaring behind her when she stopped, back still toward Sky. "And bring the two you have with you. I'd like to meet them."

Her shoulders sagged in defeat. She didn't know which was worse, showing the boys what she could really do or the fact her mother was here. She watched her walk down to the end of the hall to enter an airlock at the far end. Her sister, Myka, appeared from a hall a few feet away.

"She's pissed, you know." Myka was blonde to her dark, with white blonde hair, blue eyes and a body made for sin.

Sky threw her a frustrated look. "You think? Is it true you filed a claim?"

The blonde nodded. "It's true."

She shook her head. "Why? You never like anything about the life of a Harvester?"

Her eyes widened. "If I remember correctly, neither did you. But here you are."

"Fine." She bit out. "My ship is in lock – "

"I know – G57X – why in the hell did you pick the oldest part of the station?"

"Never mind." She turned to see Jaxon and Zane moved toward her. Jaxon had a slight limp. "What happened?"

"One of Jesata's men got a good kick in before I took him down. Nothing a massage and a warm shower won't cure." His smile gave her a sexy promise.

Unbidden a smile came to her lips. "I hear you but we've been ordered to my mother's ship within the hour. Did you get hit or anything?" The last question was directed at Zane who held a look of amazement on his face as he looked from her to her sister.

"Are all the women of your world beautiful?"

Sky frowned. "Pretty much. We all come from basically the same genetic pool with few exceptions I'm told."

"Oh, who are these fine specimens?" her sister purred.

Sky threw her sister a nasty look. "Mine. Now keep your hands off them."

"Aren't we a bitchy girl anymore?"

"Always was when you wanted to play with my things."

"Ouch." Her sister gave a pout.

Sky put her hands on her hips. "You're not going to sleep with them. Got me. I will get nasty if you even try."

Myka looked confused. "Jeez, Xera, I'm just looking for the god's sake. What's with you?" She growled at the woman she grew up with until the girl threw up her hands. "Fine. Territory spoken for...got it...be ready when I come back please." She flounced off in a huff.

Sky watched her back recede until she got to the airlock at the end before turning her attention back to her men. She let out a big sigh and knew there was so much she would need to explain in the short time they had. She felt as if all the energy drained out of her when a groan came from Jesata's way. Sky threw her a nasty look, raised her hand and the woman slumped again. "That should keep her out for a while."

Jaxon gave her a wary look. "You really get pissed off, don't you?"

"Ahhh." She walked toward the ship in a huff. She didn't need them questioning her as well. It would be bad enough to experience her mother without the woman trying to haul them all back to Tyrsati. "We need to get ready," she stated tersely and disappeared in the airlock.

She pressed the recycle key when she realized they stood at her back, touching her. "No sex right now, guys. I don't think I can handle the pressure."

"I think pressure is exactly what you need," Jaxon whispered in her ear, his hand sliding down her butt.

She groaned in response. "This really isn't the time."

"Usually isn't," Zane quipped as his hand slid around her to pinch her breasts covered in black leather.

She wanted nothing more than to curl into their hands and let them have their way. She gave a deep sigh as the door cycled open. She wiggled out of their fingers and moved to the end of the airlock closest to the ship. "You need to get over here please. Like I said, we need to prepare ourselves to visit my mother on her luxury liner." She felt them again at her back as she punched in the code to enter her ship. "Did I ever tell you what I named my ship at first?" She questioned quietly.

"No, you didn't." Zane answered as the door slid open.

She preceded them into the cabin and went to the bridge, brooding. This had not happened the way she imagined it at all. Jesata she could have handled but to have her sister and mother here on top of it all was almost too much. She flopped in the Captain's chair, lifting up the edge of her coat to look at the hole caused by the laser again. "This is going to cost me a lot to get repaired." Standing up she pulled off the coat and tossed it in the corner. It was then she noticed, Jaxon and Zane, leaning against the bulkhead. "Alright, ask, I know you're dying of curiosity."

Jaxon just moved his head side to side. "I'm not going to ask you a thing."

Zane glanced at him first before turning back to Sky. "You asked me if I knew the name of your ship out there."

Her eyes glistened. "I called it Runaway. I changed it when I got far enough from my mother. She had always told me if anyone of her girls were prepared to run away it would be me."

"Why?" He asked in a hushed voice.

She gave them a wry smile. "I guess when I was about three I packed a bag and the nanny found me on the royal grounds with a suitcase trying to find the way out." Jaxon hid his snicker behind his hand while Zane openly laughed. "It's not funny. It was right after Myka was born and I didn't understand why we had to have another baby. We were doing just fine."

"Probably because she loved your father, Sky. Just because your society was set up differently than ours, it doesn't mean your people don't care about each other." Zane walked toward her purposefully, lowering his hand to her shoulder. "Couldn't some of this be because you've misread or misunderstood the situation?"

She gave him a shocked look. "I lived there, how could I misunderstand it?"

Zane held up his hands. "Just asking." He punched a spot on the console, getting another two chairs to rise up.

Jaxon dumped himself in the other chair. "What do you need to tell us about this meeting with your mother?"

"Nothing really as it's all speculation. I'm not even sure if it's formal or not. I'm going to assume it isn't since we're in the middle of nowhere." She took in a deep cleansing breath and slowly released it. "I think you'll be good in what you have on as long as it's clean and you straighten it up." She leaned forward and put her head in her hands. What a mess...nothing they said to her would make her believe the outcome could be good...but where did that leave them? Her eyes raised and she saw they just waited, no demands, nothing but waited on her to speak.

"Bess, what's your take on the situation?"

"Geez, now you want my opinion? Plu-ea-ze!"

She looked at her hands and willed her tears away. "No school girl theatrics. I need to know what you think my chances are getting away from my mother is this time. I don't want the boys to be held because of something I did."

A long, low whistle could be heard from the computer. "You've got it bad, don't you?"

"Shut up. Calculate my chances, dammit." She continued to study her hands, as anything else would cause the emotion to overwhelm her.

"I would say they are about fifty-fifty."

Her head shot up. "Why so good?"

"Her flight plan only lead her to one place and that was here. The Quinsent docked an hour before us and from what I can gather, she plans to leave tonight. Does that sound like a person who plans to make you return home?"

Her mother was up to something, she just knew it and her mind whirled as she let out a long sigh. "You'll take them home if I can't, right?"

"Wait a minute. I can't speak for Zane but I'm staying with you even if we have to go back to your home planet." The look on Jaxon's face brooked no argument.

"I'm with him, sweetheart." Zane leaned close to her and rubbed her thigh. "We're not going to leave you for something as trivial as a family dispute. People just don't do something like that when they're mated on our planet. I'm sure it's the same for yours."

The tears spilled over and she couldn't take them back. Jaxon swung her up in his arms and walked off the bridge to her cabin to lay her gently on the bed. Zane sat on her other side. Gently, they sandwiched her between their bodies, allowing their heat to flow into her. It took a few moments before the sobs subsided and she could think coherently again. She tenderly placed a kiss on Zane's lips before turning to do the same to Jaxon.

"I don't know what's going to happen with my mother. All I can tell you is that this has been the best time of my life. I've never felt so wanted or cherished. I have you two to thank for that."

"You can thank us for the rest of our lives. We aren't leaving." Zane stated adamantly.

She placed a hand on his face. "I know you believe that but understand my mother is a powerful woman...."

"Who came here without her army. That should say something, Sky."

Jaxon's sincere look almost made her cry again. Yet, he had a point. Her mother was here mainly by herself. She couldn't be sure if her sister was here as well or even how she got here. "Excellent point."

"She might not even be here for you. Didn't you say that your sister just filed a claim here as well?"

She nodded not trusting her voice.

"Then let's go see what she has to say."

Again, she nodded then sat up. "I need to splash my face off."

"Good. We only have about fifteen minutes before your sister arrives." Zane's voice soothed her soul when she needed it most.

She got off the bed and moved to the huge bathroom. Sitting on the edge of the tub, she held a cold washcloth to her face. It wouldn't do to let her mother know she had her in tears. Just the thought of losing them made her head hurt but she had to move forward. Life would be good again, they had taught her that if nothing else. Her head went up at the soft knock.

"We only have ten minutes left. If you want us to make sure we're presentable, you'll have to let us in."

She stepped up to the door and opened it. "By all means, come in."

Zane cupped her cheek. "We'll all be alright. Have a little faith." He leaned in and kissed her mouth, his tongue sliding in then let go much too soon.

"I ditto the sentiment." Jaxon took her mouth much more forcefully, sucking on her bottom lip before invading her mouth with his tongue.

It took them less than three minutes to make sure everything was in order. Giving them all one last look, she smiled at them in the mirror. "I didn't want to say anything before but I think I'm falling in love with you two."

Two set of male arms surrounded her, pulling her tight against them. If nothing else she could remember this. She closed her eyes and committed everything about them to memory, their feel, and their touch. This was what life was supposed to be about and her resolved hardened. If she couldn't have them, she'd have no one.

Let her mother chew on that for a while.

Chapter 14

THEY WERE WAITING ON the bridge when the intercom finally beeped. Sky gave Jaxon and Zane a heartfelt look before answering. "That you, Myka?"

"Who else would it be?" came the snippy question.

She looked at the monitor and spied her sister waiting impatient at the door. "We'll be out." She stood up. "I guess this is it."

Jaxon gave her a serious stare. "We meant what we said, Sky."

"I know you do. Let me give you a little word of advice since we really didn't talk much."

"We could use that," Zane stated.

"Don't talk to my mother first. Protocol states the Queen always talks first."

"Even if she's acting in her capacity as mother?"

She nodded. "Even then in most cases. I've just seen her send lesser men to the mines for telling her their opinion. I don't want you offending her in any way. Let's go."

Walking to the door, she looked around the bridge. She hoped she'd be allowed to keep her ship. "Same security, Bess."

"See you when you get back."

That caused her heart to clench, as she didn't want to remind the ship she didn't know if she'd be returning or not. She waited patiently as the door cycled and went to meet her sister on the other side. "I hope this wasn't a formal event."

Myka grimaced at her. "Here? Are you kidding?"

She walked alongside her sister toward the Quinsent's airlock and her new prison. "You didn't say and I know how Mother is."

Her sister stopped. "You've been gone for eight year, Xera, things can change."

Confusion crossed her face. "What does that mean?"

"It means, you'll have to wait until you talk to our Mother." She continued walking toward the airlock while Sky watched her. "Are you three coming?"

Stunned that she had stopped, she ran to catch up. "Of course, we're coming. No one ignores a request from the Queen."

Myka rolled her eyes. "Give it up, will you?"

Comprehension filled her. They could never talk and this was just her way at getting back at all the nasty things she did as a child. "Fine. If you will."

She shook her head. "Already done a long time ago." She glanced back at the men. "Is she always this serious?"

"Always, ma'am," Zane answered smoothly. "Wouldn't you agree, Jaxon?"

"Absolutely, ma'am."

"Don't make me feel like an old woman, please, I'm not even into my prime yet." She gave them a wink as Sky gave her a slug. "What? I'm not allowed to get something in my eye?"

Sky glowered at her. "Just you keep those winks to yourself."

"Jealous too, isn't she, boys?"

Snickers filtered up the corridor.

Finally, they stood in front of the airlock into the Quinsent as Myka keyed in the code. All silent, they followed her into a lush hall inside the ship. "You remember your way, don't you?"

"Yes," she answered and took off to the left. She stopped, hesitated by a huge door before opening it. The room was huge and as usual, a copy of her mother's throne on Tyrsati stood at the far end. She motioned with her head for the guys to follow as she went inside. Stopping at the precise spot she remembered, she bowed deeply. "Mother."

Her Mother tapped her chin with her long finger. "Xera, this is my personal ship when not in use for official duties. You know protocol isn't necessary."

"Sorry, but Myka didn't tell me this visit wasn't official."

Her Mother let out a long sigh. "Well, when I found out my eldest was making an unscheduled visit to file a claim, I couldn't pass up the chance."

"Excuse me?" What was her Mother talking about?

"All you had to do was give me a call now and then," she drawled and indicated to the manservant beside her. "Please bring us some...," her gaze wandered back to her daughter, "...some coffee please."

Sky gasped. "How do you know about coffee?"

Her Mother rubbed her eyes for a moment before turning her gaze back to the young woman standing in front of her. "You really should have paid attention to your studies and your family history. Did nothing I told you make it into your thick skull?"

Again, snickers filtered from behind her. She whirled and glared at them. "Quiet, please." Turning back to face her mother, she answered with concern in her voice. "Mother, I learned everything you requested."

"You learned everything the council wanted you to learn. Did you learn anything I asked you to?" Frustration was evident in the woman's voice.

She cocked her head. "I – I'm not sure what you're talking about."

Her Mother shook her head. "Let's get out of this room where we can talk more privately. I think the council still has a recording device in this room. My private parlor is better. I have a scrambler in there. If you don't mind, let's retire to it."

Sky was totally confused now as to her mother's intentions and followed her meekly from the throne room. She had been in the private parlor a few times as a child but mainly stayed at home when royal duties took her Mother way. When she reached her teen years, she didn't want to go unless she was forced and never did she want to visit this room. It was here her Mother would lecture her on anything she might have done wrong.

The parlor had changed little over the years but seeing it with adult eyes made her realize just how cozy and homey the room was. There was a fireplace in the far corner with couches and chairs placed in small groupings around the room. One could blend the groups if many people were present or they could stay in place for a more intimate conversation. The walls were painted a burnt orange and she noticed there were pictures from her childhood there. Moving in closer to look at them, she was surprised to find herself in many of them. She had no memory of these being here at all.

"You were a skinny kid," Jaxon whispered near her.

She gazed at him. "I don't remember any of this."

"You do remember your father...right?"

She turned to see that her Mother had taken the lounger near the fire. "Of course, I remember him, Mother. Why wouldn't I?"

Her Mother pursed her lips. "You were quite young when he died and we never talked about it."

"I'm not sure I want to talk about it now."

The manservant came with a tray and sat it down on the table in front of her Mother. "Would you like me to serve you, your majesty?"

"Why don't you just take a break, Trey? I'll be fine here." She smiled at the man.

"As you wish."

His brilliant smile back caught Sky completely off-guard. She waited until he was out of the room. "Another lover, Mother?"

She bent over the table and poured herself a cup. "I'm old enough to do what I want, Xera. You should know that by now."

Sky blanched. "It just seemed when someone new came into the picture, you had a baby."

Her Mother's cup stopped halfway. "Thank god that can't happen anymore." She took a drink. "Just like I like it. Hazelnut I believe. Would you two like some?"

"Are you addressing my men?" she questioned.

"Interesting turn of a phrase since I was never allowed to have any of my own." Her Mother eyed her caustically. "Things weren't never quite like they appeared."

"You ran brothels! You had Harvesters bring them to you like prey." She practically screamed at her Mother.

Her Mother put her cup down. "And just how else do you propose I keep all those men safe? Sleep with them all?"

Sky blanched. She had never yelled at her Mother. "What?"

Her Mother looked at the ceiling. "Please would you all just sit down and I'll explain everything my daughter apparently never learned." She motioned to the three seats nearest her. "Regardless of what my offspring has told you, I won't bite."

Jaxon moved first. "Ma'am, Jaxon Sinclair," he said with a nod of his head.

Her Mother put out her hand to give his a firm shake. "In private, you can call me Banhi, just never in public."

Zane tossed a look over his shoulder before moving to sit next to Jaxon. "Zane Nix, ma'am." He put out this hand.

Her Mother's warm laughter filled the room. "Forward, aren't you?" She took his hand. "Strong too. Scottish, right?"

"Yes, ma'am." Jaxon agreed.

"Xera, please come and join us. You can tell me all about your mates." Her Mother patted the chair closest to her.

Reluctantly, Sky plodded to the chair and sit down. "I'm not called Xera anymore. Everyone calls me Sky."

"Fine, Sky it is." She brought her cup up to her lips again. "Want to tell me how you found Earth?"

She looked at her Mother with wide eyes. "You know about Earth?"

"If you had ever read the diary I gave you, your Father's diary by the way, you'd know the answers to all these questions." Her Mother placed her cup down on the table. "Your father came from Earth. When I went off on my own journey, I had stumbled upon the planet. I decided not to claim the planet for myself but let it live in peace. My mistake. I met a man there and we fell in love." She eyed the two men across from her. "He insisted on coming back with me to my planet. Nothing I could say would dissuade him. It was probably for the best."

"My Father came from Earth."

"He was my Father, too. At least you got to meet him." Myka's voice came from the back of the room.

"If you want part in this discussion, pull up a chair and join the group, young lady. Otherwise, you can stay back there and not say a word."

There was no denying the command in her Mother's voice. Stay or go. "I've got to hear this." Her sister's rapid tread preceded her appearance next to Sky. "Hi, you two. I'm Myka."

"Don't touch them," she warned.

"Geez, I'm not going to have sex with them, even if I wanted to...and let me tell you they are some fine specimens."

"Myka!"

Her Mother's laugh was infectious. "You haven't changed much. You still want your toys all to yourself."

She eyed the men. "And this time I can see why. Where did you all met?"

"She took us from an all-male revue, ma'am," Jaxon disclosed.

"But not before she kissed us thoroughly," Zane added. "Quite nice, I have to say."

Bright laughter filled the room yet again. "She was always a bold one. Dancers then?"

"Now. Special forces before that."

"Ah. Part of Earth's many armies. No wonder she picked you."

Sky cleared her throat. "Mother, what about my Father?"

Her Mother turned back to her. "What about him?"

"You said he came from Earth."

She nodded. "He did. I found him on an isle in a cold sea." She looked at Jaxon and Zane. "I do believe they called it Scotland."

"Right on. Isn't it beautiful?" Zane asked with a big smile.

"Focus everyone." Sky warned.

Her Mother rolled her eyes. "I did teach her politeness, I swear. Yes, it was very beautiful. We had always hoped to get back there but Andrew fell ill and died right after Myka was born."

"How could you have loved him? You kept having babies!"

Her Mother's full gaze returned to her. "They were but shabby substitutes thrust upon me by a bitter council. They all hated I had loved my mate as when they mated it was for children only. I know if I hadn't spent time on Earth I would have never learned the value of a humanoid male." She picked up her coffee again.

Sky stared at her incredulous. She had never heard this story at all. "Why all the children?"

Her Mother gave a wry nod. "Another constraint by the council. They felt if I were saddled with children I couldn't try to put the world I envisioned in place. Somehow, they made me mate with those men on my most fertile days. Hence, tons of kids."

"And the boys?"

Her Mother got a sad look. "Three of them were taken before I had a chance to remove them from the compound. I've never could find out where. I don't even want to imagine." She shuddered. "Two managed to survive because I had them transplanted in families on Earth. Still, having ten kids didn't seem to tarnish my figure any, now did it?" She ran her hand on her flat abdomen and gave a false laugh. "The council has been the bane of my existence as Queen."

"I thought Grandmother hated our Father." Myka interceded.

She shook her head. "Hated isn't the correct word. Resented would be better. Your Grandmother resented the fact I could love someone more than her. Just the fact it was a man made her angry. I thought for a while she had him killed. When I understood she didn't it was too late."

"Too late for what?"

She patted Sky's hand. "To say I was sorry for doubting her. It took me years but I finally uncovered the fact our council is the one who engineered a biochemical weapon which killed only men. I think your Father was the first casualty."

"Menos Prime," Sky breathed. "We caused that?"

Her Mother shook her head. "Not we, our Council of Twelve. They need to be deposed quickly and efficiently as well as their illicit laboratory somewhere in the Katan galaxy. I could use my oldest daughter in the fight. It's going to get very ugly," her voice ended softly.

"But what about all those men you sent to our mining colony?"

She waved her hand. "A luxury resort in Gantha."

"All of them?" Sky questioned.

Her Mother shrugged. "Unfortunately, not all of them. Some the council got before I could do anything again. Others actually deserved what they got as they were murderers." She turned her gaze to Jaxon and Zane. "I don't believe thievery is a crime if it's done to protect or feed your family. There are consequences but being placed on a mining colony isn't one of them."

"Why didn't I know this before I left?" Her skepticism never left her face.

"Would you have believed me?"

Sky knew what she said was true. She wouldn't have believed her at all. "You could have tried."

"Yes, I could have but your mentor on the council was Genda Khahn and I know how she feels about the monarchy. She always thought it was rightfully hers. I'm sure she told you you would have to take it by force."

She felt miserable. "I left because I was told I needed to kill you to take my place on the throne. She even implied you killed Grandmother."

"Genda was a new member to the council at the time, worming her way into everyone's confidence. However, she couldn't outsmart your Grandmother who knew she was dying. She staged it to look like I had taken her life even though it was the farthest thing from my mind. I loved my mother which is one of the reasons I grieved when you asked to leave."

"You understood I needed time."

Her Mother nodded. "I understood you needed time."

Myka elbowed her in the side. "See I told you it wasn't that bad."

Sky frowned at her younger sister. "Why haven't you grown up?"

"Who wants to grow up?"

She put her arm around her sister. "I wish I had stayed around a few more years. Maybe I would have been as smart as you."

"Grandmother always did say you were dense for a girl."

"That sounds like..."

Her Mother chuckled. "Bess...yes, your Grandmother wrote the original protocol for your computer. Like I said, she was a smart woman."

Sky's eyes shimmered with tears. "So, what's next?"

Her Mother opened her arms and she fell into them. "First, you're going to let me hug you. Then you'll tell me how you got so lucky and found two mates."

Epilogue

THE SUN WARMED HER back as she lay face down on a beach on an island somewhere in the South Pacific. They had decided since they were so secluded to make it a nudist beach. That was five days ago, and their honeymoon was nearly over. Sky shaded her eyes to look at them frolicking in the surf. Smiling to herself, she jumped up in all her glory and brushed off the sand.

"Oh, boys," she called seductively. "Let's go inside and have some lunch." She swung her hips seductively as she wandered up the path to the house.

Jaxon had found this place on the internet and booked it the moment they came back. True, there were a lot of loose ends to tie up with Avery Mather as well as their jobs in the revue. It all turned out well as once their commitment to her Mother was complete, they would be back for long visits and they needed their options open. Right now, they were needed on her home planet of Tyrsati to help get rid of the tyrannical Council of Twelve as well as find their illegal weapons facility.

It was a tall order but they knew they were up to it. Once her secret was out about her psionic powers, they started comparing her with some famous movie characters. Her unfamiliarity with the characters only fueled her teasing. She couldn't help it that her mind was stronger than others and she could stop bullets or lasers or toss someone across the room. She'd always had those powers, as did most from her world. There she was ordinary, here she was extraordinary.

She was fixing sandwiches when the men came in. "Hungry?"

"Only for you."

"And I'm going to take a nip right now." Zane moved behind her, putting his arms around her body to cup her breasts. "Don't you agree, nude is best?"

She got a smug look on her face. "Depends."

"She needs to be spanked again, I swear," Jaxon quipped. "But first I think I'll just eat her pussy. Hold her high, mate."

Zane lifted her up as Jaxon knelt on the floor in front of her, his lips on her cunt. His tongue licked her from stem to stern, her quiver of anticipation making her groan. This was what she was made for, she loved them and had yet to say the words.

"Today's the day, we're going to make you say it," Zane whispered.

"Nope," she answered breathless. It had become a game but one they seemed to enjoy. "Suck my clit, Jaxon, make me wet. I need both your dicks in me now."

Jaxon licked her until her juices flowed. Taking his fingers, he spread the liquid up her behind, his fingers sliding in and out of her body. Though they had only been together for a little over two months, they knew her body so well, knew how to turn her on, allowing her to take the most pleasure from her body.

"She's ready, Zane. Let me slid in first. I'll hold her." Jaxon stood, put his arms under her knees and entered her in one fluid motion.

She grunted. "That feels so good."

He leaned back on the counter and presented her ass to Zane. "You're turn, mate."

Zane bent forward. "Are you ready for this?"

"Always," she whispered.

He rammed into her from behind and her fulfillment was complete. Slowly, they both began to move in her, building the tension within her body, their hands stroking each other and her. She felt safe and secure between them as they pushed her body to higher heights.

"Please – please – rub me. Faster. Harder." Her breath came out in hard pants. She was close and she hoped they were too.

Then deliberately, they slowed down their motion. "Let's take her to the couch." Zane suggested.

She was so close, yet they teased her as Jaxon carried her to the couch, his cock still in her.

"Zane's going to get on the bottom, lass. You'll really feel his big dick then."

She gasped. Zane was bigger around than Jaxon and a tighter fit but he drove her wild the way he moved his hips. "That will – "

"Be a little tight?" he asked. "Better for me to get off, my dear." Her whole body trembled as she remembered the last time she was in that position. She had lost control and almost passed out. Zane lay on the couch and raised his hands. "Looks like I need to work on you again. Jax, can you hold her up a little longer?"

"No problem, man, she's as light as a feather."

Zane swooped in with his tongue to lick her anus and she surged against Jaxon. "Seems like I hit a hot spot." Continuing his perusal with his tongue, he licked where they joined, grasping his balls in a slight grip, making Jaxon grow inside her even more. "How do you like that big boy? Should I turn you around and put my finger up your ass?"

The big man trembled. "It's your turn next, buddy, let's just finish her first."

"Finish her it is." His fingers rimmed her tight rosette before searing it once more with this tongue. "Can you feel me? Are you sensitive?" His thumb moved around the tight area before dipping inside. "How does that feel? Do you want my dick there?"

"Yes," she groaned. "Your big hard cock needs to be in me now."

"Looks like the princess is rather demanding today." Jaxon leaned forward to Zane, giving him a hard kiss. "Should we make her wait any longer?"

Zane returned the kiss. "I don't know what do you think?"

Sky twitched in his arms. "Dick in me. Now." Her breath came out in ragged gasps.

"As long as I can do it slow."

"I don't care. I just need to feel you both."

Zane stroked his dick one final time. "Set her on me nice and slow, Jaxon. I want her to feel my whole nine inches."

"You got it."

He lowered her and she felt Zane's hand on her, guiding her tight anus toward his hard cock. It took a minute before her tight sphincter would give so he could push himself fully inside her. Once inside, she let out a long, unhurried sigh and rocked her hips a little. Reaching up, she pulled Jaxon's mouth to hers, kissing him deeply.

"Now fuck me you two."

In and out, they moved in a natural rhythm pushing her to higher heights. When she thought she would take the plunge, Jaxon pulled back and plucked her clit. She thought she would pass out, the pleasure was so intense. She heaved forward to rub herself against his huge cock as Zane pounded her from behind.

The buildup was like an erotic flame, flickering and gaining strength until it would burn itself out in a glowing ember. The heat was strong and suddenly, she was an inferno, her movements frenzied. It was better than anything she had ever felt as she cried out her joy, her bliss as they took her over the edge only lovers can. Within seconds, they had joined her calling out her name in sheer abandonment.

Sated, their limbs mingled together as they sandwiched her yet again on the small couch. "I love you, Jaxon. I love you, Zane." She could have sworn they heard their cries of happiness on Tyrsati.

••••✳•••

Award winning author **Lynn Crain** has done it all in her life. From nursing to geology, her life experiences have added to her detail rich stories. She loves writing full time as she weaves contemporary, fantasy, futuristic and paranormal tales, tame to erotic, for various publishers. Her home is in the desert southwest and she's just returned from her latest adventure of living in Vienna, Austria while her husband worked his dream job. She loves hearing from her readers at lynncrain@cox.net.

Website
http://lynncrain.blogspot.com/

Amazon Author Page
http://www.amazon.com/Lynn-Crain/e/B00VNP03TE/

..•• ✳ •••.

Praise for Lynn Crain's Books:

"This is a wonderful short read. Crain does a first rate job of describing the smells and sounds of the era, the smell of burning coal from the train etc. I felt with each description that I was there in that time period experiencing it for myself. She does an equally good job of portraying life on a small remote island, circa 1830s. I'd definitely recommend this one." ~ The Haunting of Maggie Grey ~ 4 Cherries

"In the final book of the Blue Moon Series, Lynn Crain tells an explosive story that had me on the edge of my seat! From Connor's emergence as Charles Langford's son, to the battle between Connor and Cordelia, the imagery and fast pace made this one a true page-turner. The sex between these two lovers was white hot, but the ending so very romantic as they vowed their love. Blue Moon Magic 4: Night of the Blue Moon, like its predecessors, is a keeper. I am only sad now that the series has ended." ~ Night of the Blue Moon ~ 4.5 Lips

"The love scenes incorporated tenderness and need, without the intense erotic raunchiness I expect from an erotic romance. And that fit A View from Santa's Sleigh so much better than anything else would have. Throw in some truly interesting, and sometimes funny, secondary characters, and A View from Santa's Sleigh made a great read. In my mind, there are several categories of great romances, and this one is towards the top of my "Sweet Romances" list. I'm hoping to see some of the secondary characters with stories of their own." ~ The View From Santa's Sleigh ~ 4 Hearts

"Lynn Crain does a wonderful job of creating characters that are likeable, intelligent and in need of acceptance, love, change and self-discovery." ~ Joyfully Reviewed

"Lynn Crain offers another great story filled with a fantasy world existing beneath the ancient rocks of Stonehenge. It's a tale that will appeal to those who enjoy Merlin lore, fairies, wizards, and the magic of Stonehenge." ~ Amazon Reader Review

"Lynn Crain delivers another scorching hot story to heat up your winter nights. Run-don't walk-to grab this 99 cent ebook and settle in for a satisfying story of fairies, magic and a sexy wizard who will steal Rachel's heart." ~ Amazon Reader Review

"In the final book of the Blue Moon Series, Lynn Crain tells an explosive story that had me on the edge of my seat! Who would have thought that Charlie's son was not dead? The fight between Cordelia and Connor I could really see in my mind as the pages were eagerly read. The sex between this pair was white hot and I fought with Cordelia and Connor as they went on a rescue mission, but the ending was so romantic as they vowed their love to one another. Blue Moon Magic: Night of The Blue Moon is a keeper as well as the other books, however I am now sad that the series has ended." ~ Goodreads Review

.••• ✳ •••.

Awards:

2011 EPIC's eBook Winner for Erotic Historic Romance

2010 Realizing the Dream Winner at the Desert Dreams Conference

2009 LRC Finalist

You can find more Lynn Crain books at:

www.extasybooks.com
www.devinedestinies.com
www.lynncrain.com
www.lynncrain.blogspot.com

...●●● ✳ ●●●...

Bonus Material

Brought to you

by

And

Lynn Crain

Dive into the new supernatural world of The JR Chronicles from award-winning author, Lynn Crain. Here she will bring the first short story during the time heroine, Serenity Donovan, is learning her trade of paranormal investigator. Next, she will bring you part of Serenity's diary, kept during her learning curve into the paranormal world.

If you'd like e-book copies of these two free stories in The JR Chronicles world, please check Lynn's blog at www.lynncrain.blogspot.com or her Facebook author page at www.facebook.com/LynnCrainAuthor.

Spring's
PESKY IMP

A JR CHRONICLES SHORT

LYNN CRAIN

Welcome to Spring, Nevada. It's a historic silver mining town very close to Sin City filled with historic homes, horrible track houses and the inevitable mansions of the wealthy casino execs not wanting to live there. Right now, it's being terrorized by an imp. Yup, right in the middle of the town square where it's scaring the natives as they wait for the bus to Vegas. And it's right up my alley as my hereditary job requires I rid the town of its presence. Yup, that's me, Serenity Donovan, paranormal investigator to the rescue. Wonder what my sidekick will say...did I mention he's a ghost?

Spring's Pesky Imp

I'm SURE YOU THINK THIS is about the season. It isn't. It's all about the imp who was terrorizing those who waited for the Vegas bus in the town square of Spring, Nevada.

Spring should have been a ghost town by now but with its proximity to Sin City and mountains still loaded with silver, it had managed somehow to limp into the 21st century. Today, strewn amongst the historic homes, there were track houses along with the inevitable mansions of the wealthy, none who were famous beyond the borders of Nevada. Many casino execs didn't want their families in the city and came to Spring to live their idyllic dream in a small town.

But today isn't even about the imp. It's about my ability to make it go away, leave the fair people of my hometown to their own devices and therefore, none the wiser for the supernatural event happening in their midst.

I was very happy that George had come over and substantiated the rumors I heard. Something wasn't quite normal in the city square. There had been descriptions of scaly skin, a wide face and lots of scary teeth. I'd have to look at footage and make sure but I was fairly confident from the descriptions it was an imp. Then again, they were notoriously fast and I might not even get a glimpse from the digital feed at all, even in slow-mo.

I carefully packed what I needed in my pockets including a shopping bag and a second-hand purse I'd found especially for this task. It was during this packing that Jasper decided to show. The air cooled and slowly he appeared next to me. To some, he would seem an apparition but in a few minutes he'd be as solid as you or I.

"What are you doing?" Apparition or not, his voice was deep and very sure of himself.

"What does it look like?" His scent embraced me, clean and woodsy, as if he'd been out walking out behind the house in the pine trees along with aspen and various other trees.

He let out a soft sigh. "If I knew, I wouldn't ask."

I arched a brow and scrunched my face. "I would have thought you'd been listening to my conversation with George yesterday."

He stared at me with his blue eyes, face shadowed and not showing any emotion. By now, he was totally solid and I tried not to notice just how handsome he was. "I was otherwise occupied."

"Oh." On a normal day, he would practically be in my back pocket, so there wasn't much to say. "He said there have been reports of people sighting something in the square."

"Any ideas?"

I lifted a shoulder. "Maybe."

His scowl made me want to laugh. "That's informative."

"Scaly skin, big teeth and a wide grin. And that's when you can see it at all. It has been stealing then returning some parts of what it stole."

"Imp." No hesitation there.

I nodded once. "My impression as well."

"And your solution?" Always the teacher.

I held up the dilapidated satchel purse and the bag of food. I didn't tell him that I had a new phone in my pocket to hopefully record the event as he'd just think it was a waste of money. Times change and my thoughts were the more technology, the better. "A purse full of things that only an imp could love and a bag of food. All imbibed with a spell that makes it see the error of its ways."

I felt proud of my deductions as I'd looked in the ancestors journals and found that Grandma Jess had one in the same area in the 1950s before my mother was born. She'd concluded then that he wasn't the vicious type but just trying to get some attention because he was lonely. From the current incidents with this one, I could almost conclude the same thing. I'd just have to touch it to be sure. It might even be the same one.

"I suppose I should come with you." His voice dripped with reluctance.

"Don't let me put you out or anything." I shoved my house keys in my jeans pocket without the new phone.

"Did you remember a mirror?"

I stopped mid-stride. I'd made it to the hall and let out a sigh. So what if I'd forgot an important part of the spell. I needed to look into its eyes for it to feel the full effect of the spell. Going to the credenza by the front door, I rummaged through my own bag there until the required item was found. "Does it matter if it's rectangular or round?"

"Not that I recall." He shrugged into his jacket as he came up the hall.

"I guess that means you're coming with me?"

"Sure but I'll be invisible before we get to the end of the lane." He noted my jacket as well. "Walking or driving?"

"Walking." A slight breeze ruffled the papers in the corner as I opened the door. City square was just a brisk fifteen minute walk from my home and my need for exercise in the January sunshine great. I breathed in the fresh mountain air and was thankful Spring was far above the valley floor where Vegas resided. The climate overall was temperate and pleasant most of the year. We had more rain than some places in Nevada but averaged only a few weeks of cold weather each year. And we rarely had a temp over ninety in the summer.

The air today was cool and my cheeks responded. It was exhilarating as I walked down the lane toward my destination. My 3-G Grandmother Myrtle had purchased this house and land with money made right here in the local mines. Then her husband died and she was left alone with three young children.

I had started earlier in the month to read her journal of the time. The women in my family, from the moment they got here, had been protectors of the town to the best of their ability. At least one daughter had followed the path and since I had been my parents' only child, I'd inherited the mantle.

"You're thinking about them." The words gentle and not condescending.

"I'm allowed to think." I didn't want him to think me weak or unworthy of my calling.

"Yes, but don't dwell. Your mother wouldn't have wanted that."

My throat tightened and I gave a quick nod. My parents had died in a car accident last fall, so the wound was fresh and raw. I cleared my mind because all my wits would be needed for the imp. I was so new to doing this stuff alone. I knew both Jasper and George worried about me but at the moment they didn't know each other. At least not personally.

"I'll be right here."

I turned to thank him but he was already gone. I pursed my lips and took a left by the big oak tree. It was very old and there were many days as a child I'd throw my arms around it in hopes of gaining its wisdom. It hadn't happened yet.

It took me another ten minutes and I found myself staring across a wide span of grass with parking all around. In the 1950s, while trying to revitalize the community, someone got the bright idea that the town needed a square just like many mid-western towns.

One side housed the library and police station that had taken over the next city block as well. There was even talk of them building a new library then the police could have that whole side of the square.

The portion opposite those buildings held a bowling alley, a sit-down and our local credit union. All were also editions from the 1950s. The part directly opposite me, what I considered the top of the square, housed the old elementary school. It had turned into city hall when the new school was built a couple of miles away in the mid-70s. It was called a bicentennial school like every other school built that year in Nevada. My Mom had graduated then and loved the moniker given to the place.

The side where I walked in, there was an antique shop, a now defunct dress shop and a realty. All streets around the square boxed it in and there were a few streets that came in at the corner angles. All it all, it was very homey and looked nothing like Sin City just over the hill.

Every place on the square had a view of the bus benches that sat facing the sit-down. The credit union had the second best view while the bowling alley mainly saw the bushes and trees. All the other businesses, include the police station, got a view from a distance.

No one occupied the benches today. I was able to sit down with little fanfare and hopefully, no one cared to watch. I was fooling myself by even thinking lack-of-interest as everyone seemed to be busy bodies here. This part of town remained untouched over all. Sure, a couple of blocks over there were some exclusive hotels and supposedly the one where Jasper – I stopped myself short. There was no reason for me to think of that right now. The imp was the item on the agenda today.

I pulled my new phone out of my pocket and began recording the scenery, taking in what I could from my view on the bench. It was my hope that every event would be documented with video as well as pictures. And I just need to figure out to catalogue them for easy access.

After about an hour, I was getting bored. No one else had stopped by at all and frankly, I didn't blame them as it seemed the bus wasn't running on time yet again. Out of the corner of my eye, I saw something small, gray-green and scaled. Turning my full attention toward the end of the bench, there was nothing there.

"Don't forget the mirror," a voice whispered close to my ear.

As casually as I could, I pulled the mirror from my pocket and turned it in such a way where I could see the purse and food bag. Soon a pair of longish ears, scaled in green and white appeared, followed immediately by a set of gray bloodshot eyes.

"I've got you now." It looked up startled but my gaze caught its eyes as it tried to slither away. "No, you don't."

I kept the mirror in place and reached around to grab it by its scruff.

I pulled it to stand in front of me as I allowed my other hand to touch it more fully. Waves of loneliness flowed from it. It had craved attention and whatever had been keeping it in the forest was gone. I couldn't tell exactly if that were another spell or something else. I allowed kindness and feelings of safety, belonging along with love flow from me.

I'd never gave during a reading before but I could sense when there would be times I'd need to do just that. After a few minutes, he finally relaxed though I was a little surprised when it identified itself as male since they tended to be more negative and harder to keep corralled by spellcraft.

Soon, he chatted away while looking through his bag of goodies. He made a happy sound when he found the oranges and five-pound bag of trail mix. Definitely the boy my Grandma Jess had harnessed.

Still chattering, he found the side pocket where I'd put my card. This time I took his hand.

"You can come talk to me anytime. No more scaring people."

He eyed me cautiously. *"You're like her you know."*

Curiosity was high. *"Like who?"*

"Your mother. The spell only held me so long because of her visits. She'd leave presents."

Obviously I'd need to read my mother's journals first and maybe work my way from both ends. *"Sorry, I didn't know."*

"'S okay. Where is she? I'd love to talk to her." An unexpected wave of sorrow flowed from me. *"No. When?"*

"Last fall." We sat there quietly for a few moments. *"Any place special I need to drop off your supplies at?"* I finally managed.

He watched me a moment, feelings flowing deep in his gray eyes as he tried to convey them to me. *"The clearing next to Tyler Falls is usually where we met."* His rough fingers touched my wrist. *"I'll take you to some of the places she thought special."* And then he was gone.

I concentrated on my breathing because I wanted to scream and pitch a fit. It just wasn't fair. A tear slipped down my cheek followed by another then another until it was a constant flow. "Did you know?" I questioned, my voice raspy.

"I suspected but wasn't sure." I could feel his warm breath on my neck. Ghosts don't breathe so obviously he was trying comfort me. "We have company."

I raised tear-filled eyes to see George coming our way from the police station. I brushed my face with the back of my hand and tried to smile brightly but even I knew it fell flat.

He stood in front of me for a moment, his gaze not missing a thing. "Are you all right?"

I shook my head and tried hard to keep the emotion out of my voice. "He knew my mother."

George sat down with a thud, his arm going around my shoulder. "You did good, kid, you did good."

And wait...there's even more bonus material for you...

Ever wonder what my life was like before I became Spring's only paranormal investigator? Let me take you back through my transition between then and now. We'll start at the very beginning, right after my parents died, when I was wading through things I didn't understand well because of my lack of training. That's right...I documented every day, every moment...of how I became me. Exciting, isn't it?

．．．● ✳ ●．．．

January 2009

1 ~ Mom always said I should take notes and I guess today's the day I start. I miss her. I miss her telling me what to do, how to handle JR and...well...just everything. Not much of a way to start a new business, is it?

2 ~ Second day and the phone hasn't made a sound. Did Mom have to wait this long?

3 ~ I'm telling you. I'm going crazy. I mean who wouldn't in my position. I have been studying for this since I can remember. And that's not all I can remember. The number one thing on that list...meeting Jasper Ryan or JR for short depending on my mood...I mean, it's not every day a girl meets a ghost and then gets told he will always be her partner. Geez...I was only nine when I first saw him...glad I never told my Mom then. I'm sure she'd be smacking me on my head for thinking he's hot now. Actually more than hot. How about incredible?

4 ~ Other than drooling over JR again, da nada. How many ways can one say nothing?

5 ~ Another day of nothing.

6 ~ How about this for the word nothing? Zippo.

7 ~ Da Nada. Must do a word study sometime.

8 ~ Phone has been ringing off the hook but it's those wicked salesmen again. I know that their jobs must be hell and in today's economy it must be really tough. Thank goodness that Mom and Dad left me well off. Still, I'd hex those telemarketers if I knew it wouldn't come back on me.

9 ~ Trying to deal with life makes me want to be a kid again. Heck, I am a kid but I know I'm different. And not in a special way. I know that I have a job to do for this world and that's to keep everyone safe from those supernatural things they don't understand. I don't care what your age is, that would be a heavy burden for anyone. Still, I'd love to see my Mom and Dad and just get on with the things a kid is supposed to do. Know what I mean?

10 ~ Hope neither Mom nor the ancestors care what my journal looks like. As I stand in the library and gaze around me, I see all the ones that my foremothers wrote. They're all bound leather with wonderful covers in many styles and colors. I just bought twelve of the same composition books – guess there's a little of my Dad in me. At least they look new age with a faux paper design and multiple colors. That's good...right?

·•● ✳ ●•·

11 ~ The Olsen's down the street just called. Good thing I'm a night owl. Apparently, their dog is barking at what appears to be nothing uncontrollably. They think I should come and check it out. JR is coming with me just in case it's something I can't handle. Apparently, he's tied to me instead of the house. Or maybe it's a little of both but that's an issue to explore later. For now, on to the Olsens and their dog. It's just a dog. And probably there's a cat lurking in the shadows. Besides, their house has always been locked up tight like a prison. At least, that's what Jody used to tell me when we were in high school. Wonder what she's been up to recently? Heard she's gone away to college but she's never kept in touch.

12 ~ Wow. My first real paranormal event. The thing that Mr. Olsen didn't tell me when he was on the phone was that he and his wife were trapped in the kitchen. Their dog wouldn't let them out of it and it was like the animal went all Cujo on them. But the dog had his reasons. Of course, it goes without saying that it was a ghost but not your regular run-of-the-mill type since it had no tie to the house or a person like JR does. But it was apparent, it had ties to the land, as it was a native from many years ago. The entity felt so horrible that the Olsen's were scared out of their wits. While Jasper dealt with the entity, I consoled the Olsen's, did a little mumbo-jumbo so it appeared that I did something when in reality, JR took care of this one for me. I did have to break the news to them that the dog had been digging up the very back of their property and the ghost wanted to chastise the dog because of it. While it wasn't a burial ground or anything, apparently, the local shaman from about 500 years had buried something bad there. He wouldn't tell JR just what it was but he did tell us that

we all needed to stay away. I learned long ago to listen to those who are wiser than myself. The Olsen's should too.

13 ~ I should be studying the journals left for me. There's a reason they are here and I've been told that anything I could ever run up against will be in their pages somewhere. But I felt a little odd when I picked up my Great-great-great-Grandmother Lyttle's leather bound diary. It gave me a funny little zap when I put my hand on it. At first I pulled back but whatever ward is there, it wasn't meant to keep me away. It's almost as if it's drawing me nearer...

14 ~ How many ways are there to say nothing? Here's one: niets. Yes, I'm starting that different languages search because I am bored out of my mind. And this is with studying the journals. Mom was always busy...what's wrong with me?

15 ~ And yet another way. Kein ding.

16 ~ And another. Nulla

17 ~ Really? A cat in a tree? That's the best you can do?

18 ~ About that cat. It's still up there and any time the firemen get close, the darn thing gets nasty. Maybe I should go look at it to see what's going on. At least this one is just a few doors down from my painted lady. Late Entry – The cat had nothing wrong except the fact the owner's son wasn't being nice to it. All I had to do was to touch it to pick that one up. The owner wasn't happy about the issue but I told her if the kid didn't stop, I'd

make sure the cat went to the animal shelter in hopes of getting a better home. Somehow, I think the poor thing will be coming to see me more since I'm only two houses away.

+

19 ~ Now, this is more like it. They want me to do a reading. The person is dead but I really think it will help me hone my skills as they do need work. The Force actually needs to know if it was foul play or not.

20 ~ Well, after yesterday's debacle at the funeral home, I guess they won't be calling me back for a while. People really shouldn't ask me what the dying man's thoughts and words were if they really didn't want to know. Guess 'I'm coming' wasn't what the wife expected. How was I to know he wasn't with her? Is that a form of foul play?

21 ~ Why is a Spring Gazette reporter calling me? If someone at that funeral home has been talking, they will regret it. Well – maybe not – I don't want Mom rolling in her grave nor it coming back on me threefold. Do you think growling would work? Besides I really didn't know that Spring still had adultery in the books as a crime. Thought that went out of vogue a long time ago. After all we are next to Vegas.

22 ~ Jasper has been awfully quiet recently. Wonder what's up with that.

23 ~ Apparently, yesterday was his first day at Myrtle's boarding house in 1872. He says there are definitely times when he sees that ancestor in me. I'm going to make a promise to myself to read all the

ancestors diaries as I've just been doing it hit and miss. I've been told this house and the ancestors have seen everything. The knowledge just might come in handy sometimes and prevent any surprises on my part. Like the one that happened with that dead guy. Never again.

24 ~ There was a mewing at the door this morning. Guess I called that one right. She says she has a lot more to tell me and wants to know if she can stay with me. What am I supposed to say to that one? I mean, Mrs. Keiper does care for the cat and if the scolding the boy got while I was there was any indication, there won't be another incident. Still, there's something about this kitty. She tells me her name is Shade.

25 ~ Jasper says that Shade reminds him of the cat 3-G-Grandma Lyttle had. It's funny how the little piece of calico fluff flips her tail at him then gives a little half-smirk. He says I'm reading too much into it. I think she's been here during a past life. Yeah, they really do have nine according to my mother. Note about the 3-G reference for future readers so they understand what I mean...well...that's my abbreviation for the number of greats before the word grandmother. So, 3-G-Grandma Lyttle is my Great-great-great-grandmother Lyttle. The abbreviation makes it much easier.

26 ~ I'm looking at old photos in the library here at home. It's amazing just how much all of us look alike. I can see where Jasper says that I'm like 3-G-Grandma Lyttle, at least in the size category. But it's hard to tell from these pictures since they are just black and white. It's more like a cream color and maybe shades of gray. I think that Mom had them redone and colorized. I'll have

to find them to see exactly what the resemblance is. Maybe it's the facial structure but I swear, I don't see a thing. Late entry – OMG! Maybe I should have said OMFG as I swear if my hair is truly that color, I'm going to cut it all off.

27 ~ I'm back at it in the library and Jasper says that our hair color is just about the same. I'm hoping the look on my face helped discouraged him from saying more. It's not on the agenda to discuss if I'm like my ancestor in coloring or not. I'll just leave it to my stylist if I ever get one. Right now, I'm concentrating on what 2-G-Grandma Dora did to get rid of an imp. Looks like there might be one downtown and people are telling me about it. I'll have to wait until George calls though because of the funeral home issue. I don't even know if they'll call me but a girl can be hopeful, can't she?

28 ~ Yup, it appears to be an imp, mischievous creatures that they are. Apparently, there are pranks being done to people who are waiting for the Vegas bus in the town square. People at first thought they were being punked, but by who I have no idea, since no one famous seems to come here at all, then someone saw him. Ugly bugger was the words they apparently used with George. He thought I was getting bored and though he wasn't supposed to call me, he dropped by and suggested that I just go sit at the square for a while once I did some studying. Maybe I'll just do that.

29 ~ This imp has some issues and though he isn't malevolent, he certainly isn't going to stop anytime soon from what I gleaned from the previous journals. Apparently, from the looks of the police reports that

George managed to bring me today, he's done this for about a week now with a variety of people. Most of them ended up terrified. I'm sure when one sees a gremlin, one doesn't quite want to believe it. I'm off to read some past accounts of how the ancestors dealt with this issue. I'm hoping the resolution will be gentle and painless. Late Entry – Found the perfect thing in Grandma Jess's journal. She got rid of one back in the late '50s by putting a spell on an object the imp stole. And that is very similar to what this one is doing. So far he's taken a bag of groceries then returned it with a bite taken out of everything in the bag. He took a briefcase, a purse and just about anything sat on the bench next to the person who owned it. So either this little guy has run out of places to shop and is in need or he is intensely lonely.

30 ~ So far, so good. I went to the bench yesterday and sat down, placing both a used satchel full of items and a recently purchased bag of groceries next to me. It wasn't long before I saw his gnarled hand reach up and snatch them both but I caught him good with my mirror, so I could get to the bottom of his issues. We also talked and I found out he knew my mother well. The spells placed on them were pretty innocent. The food though good gave him a vibe of doing better out in the hills surrounding the town than in the square. The satchel gave him the thought that he needed nothing else to make him happy. I tried to put things in it that only an imp would love: broken jewelry, a doll, and my business card as I know he'll become lonely someday. It's better for him to visit me than to make himself a nuisance to the townspeople.

31 ~ Wow, I made it a whole month journaling. Even Jasper's impressed. He thought nothing could hold my attention for this long. Why does he see me as such a kid? I may never find out.

www.ingramcontent.com/pod-product-compliance
Lightning Source LLC
Chambersburg PA
CBHW050940120626
46552CB00001B/300